THE
CITY
OF
LOST
DREAMERS

Also by Lisa Lueddecke

A Shiver of Snow and Sky
A Storm of Ice and Stars
The Forest of Ghosts and Bones

THE
CITY
OF
LOST
DREAMERS

LISA LUEDDECKE

■SCHOLASTIC

Published in the UK by Scholastic, 2021
Euston House, 24 Eversholt Street, London, NW1 1DB
Scholastic Ireland, 89E Lagan Road, Dublin Industrial Estate, Glasnevin,
Dublin, D11 HP5F

SCHOLASTIC and associated logos are trademarks and/or
registered trademarks of Scholastic Inc.

ISBN 978 1407 19664 0

A CIP catalogue record for this book is available from the British Library.

Printed by CPI Group (UK) Ltd, Croydon, CR0 4YY
Paper made from wood grown in sustainable forests and other controlled
sources.

1 3 5 7 9 10 8 6 4 2

This is a work of fiction. Names, characters, places, incidents and dialogues
are products of the author's imagination or are used fictitiously. Any
resemblance to actual people, living or dead, events or locales is entirely
coincidental.

www.scholastic.co.uk

For my sisters,
Cynthia, Rebekah, Diana and Heidi.

"The words 'far, far away' had always
a strange charm."

ALFRED, LORD TENNYSON

Prologue

From A *History of Shard*
by Lyuba Genova, 3A 96

And the city, in its glory
Sat by two crossing rivers
Turrets high among the clouds
Windows silver slivers.
And from a hundred miles far
In hills that stood as guards,
One could see its lustrous form,
Saying, "There sits mighty Shard."

So wrote Nedda, one of the Great Enchanters, describing the gem of Sarsova that is the City of Shard. A beacon of hope and trade to the kingdom, its existence burned hot and bright, before its light was extinguished.

When a number of dreygas, the vampire-like creatures known to feed on magic, were found to be roaming the city, the most powerful enchantress of us all, Baba Yaga, used her boundless magic to tie the city's essence to a map, which she then tore into three pieces and flung into the wind. And with it went the city, wandering invisible and ripped away from the world. Cursed to roam about Sarsova without ever being seen.

The dreygas should have been no match for the Guild. An issue easily dealt with. No one knows why Baba Yaga decided to banish the city rather than leave the Guild to vanquish the dreygas. It remains one of the great mysteries of Shard.

But the magic of the curse could not be undone, and only if those pieces of the map find their way back to one another can the city ever return to Sarsova.

In the days that followed, the queen of the City of Shard, Queen Ulyana, together with her husband, retreated into the palace with their young daughter, never to be seen again. The Guild settled into their place as the rulers of the city, mapping old gardens and empty plots into fields where grain could grow. Settling unrest when and where it flared to life. Working, always, to save the city. To undo a curse that ripped hope away from entire generations.

To return us all to Sarsova.

1

Before the city had been cursed to wander, people said the wind would whistle down the streets like a giant whistling on its way home. Loud and sharp and inescapable. I tried to imagine it each day as I traipsed down the busy streets, thinking about the before. The old days, before our city was ripped away from the rest of the kingdom. When we were still a part of the world outside – ten years before I was born. I would imagine I could feel the wind hastening from distant mountains, bringing snow and ice and darkness with it.

But those days were as gone as the dead. There was no wind in Shard any more. No snow or ice or stars to beat back the darkness. There was just the city, and then nothing. If you opened the gates and looked out at the beyond, you'd be greeted by an endless swathe of brownish grey that looked remarkably like dishwater. Not a single discernible object to be seen anywhere. Not a hint of a blue sky. Not a scrap of green. Just a colourless maw of emptiness, stretching away for ever.

I pulled open the doors of the Guild and slipped inside, the bustle of the city streets dying suddenly away.

I had heard that when you entered the Guild headquarters – the Mappers' Guild, officially, but no one called it that – you could *feel* the map magic simmering in the air. That it clung to your senses like a candle had just been blown out. I always took a moment when I first arrived, to take it in, to breathe, to close my eyes and see if I could feel it too. To see if I had somehow missed that magic lurking somewhere deep inside me. But I never felt a thing.

I let out a sharp breath and stomped across the grand foyer. Hanging above me, in an ornate frame, was a tiny scrap of the map. The Guild had found this piece of Baba Yaga's curse map many years ago, and had kept it safe here in the Guild, displaying it to anyone who passed through. They were always on the hunt for the other two pieces, so they could return the city to Sarsova. Scouts and hunters silently scoured the city for any sign of them, but so far, to no avail.

I didn't bother glancing up at it.

Instead, I made my way to the side room where my little dusty desk sat waiting for a day of unimaginable boredom. Already, a stack of citations sat waiting to be filed, and letters that weren't for me sat waiting to be delivered. A small sign that said *Clerk* hung askew outside the door.

The crooked sign wasn't even mine. *I wasn't even a Clerk.* I was a trainee who did the jobs that the Clerks found too dull. I fancied ripping the sign off the wall and stomping it to pieces for the way it looked at me – taunted me – but no need to make a scene so early in the day. That could at least wait until lunch.

I took a step forward. Stopped. Tried again.

No. No. No. No. No. I couldn't face the day just yet. I turned on my heel and made my way down the hallway with long, slow steps. The filing could wait. If I kept my pace slow, I could wander up and down every hallway on the ground floor of the Guild and circle back to the office having killed half an hour.

In the world outside the small room where I spent most of my day, life buzzed. Guild members – all deliciously full of magic that I would never get to know – moved about the various floors. Classes full of Charges wound on, teachers' voices bursting forth from partially closed doorways, some students running late and scurrying through the doors with armfuls of books from the Atheneum – the expansive library that took up half of the Guild and housed the entrance to the mysterious Sanctum. There were rooms with closed doors, muffled voices emanating from within and beckoning for me to listen, cloaked Magisters going in and out and hastily closing the door again.

Back in the Very Old Days, long before the city was sent wandering, there were many more types of magic than just map magic. But, as wars broke out, and magic and magicless people began to clash, it was eventually decided that magic must be governed by language and words. Sketched out and designed on paper before ever being spoken to life by an incantation. If you wanted a new building, you had to sketch it out and match it with words. If you wanted to make a door disappear, you had to draw the wall without the door. It helped to keep magic very precise, but it still left enough room for mistakes.

The older types of magic were deemed unsafe. Sometimes people still whispered about them – curse magic, or medical magic – but over time, they had all been washed away. Memories of how to perform them faded with time. Map magic was useful. Helpful. Mostly safe, and with many uses. It was good and right, and everything that magic was meant to be. Or that's what everyone said, anyway.

Outside my tiny office, the world of map magic flourished.

Inside the room, the wilted plant in the corner was a fitting illustration of how I felt: withered. Faded. Dull. Every day I left feeling empty and exhausted. I would go to bed feeling a small spark of optimism that tomorrow, something would change. Tomorrow, my true life would start. The life I dreamed was mine, rich and alive. I would learn that I truly *did* have map magic, perhaps; or I would stumble upon an adventure while out on an errand for the Guild. Gods, if only. I needed something to change. *Needed it*. I had read enough books in my stolen moments in the Atheneum to know that anything was possible. But *likely* was another story entirely.

My walk through the Guild ended all too soon. My small office stood before me again. As did the dead plant, and the cluttered desk, and the stack of citations.

Dust rose on the thick air when I sat down heavily. I sneezed.

Perhaps I should just go home now. The day had started poorly, and if I was being honest, was it likely to improve?

"Siya."

My head snapped up. Official Fredek stood in the doorway, a copy of *Map Magic and the City of Shard: An Official City Code* tucked under one arm. I stood quickly, sending the stack of citations fluttering on to the floor. Frustration seared through me, and came out in a snarled smile.

"Good morning." I tried in vain to catch a few of the fluttering citations before they reached the ground.

"I'm afraid you'll have to do your filing later."

Oh no. That's too bad.

"I need you to accompany me and a Charge on a house call. This one can't wait."

A house call! Going outside! Now I was interested.

"What happened?" I asked.

"An unauthorized cellar enhancement has ended with the owner stuck inside. No door. Could leave him down there a while longer to teach him a lesson, but best not to. Don't want to upset the higher-ups." His eyes darted upwards, to the upper levels of the Guild, where eminent Magisters worshipped the rules of magic as though deities themselves.

The rules were *everything* to them. That was understandable. When people didn't follow the rules, it could have catastrophic results. Unauthorized map magic that had ultimately failed in some way usually required cleaning up by the Guild. I rarely got to attend those visits, but occasionally when the other clerks were busy, I would get to go.

"Of course not." Disappearing doors were a common issue in the city. If the door was gone, the wall was sealed by magic, and there was no way out until someone like Official Fredek or one of the highly skilled Magisters came and freed the unlucky party. A hefty fine and a slap on the wrist was the best-case scenario. Being stuck there for ever was the worst.

Although that rarely happened. There were stories of the occasional magician vanishing, lost in a botched mapping attempt that saw them never return home – but they might have just been stories. Mapping required careful time and attention. Drawing out the plan on parchment and matching it to an incantation. One wrong step, and a whole lot could go wrong.

He sniffed. "Shall we?"

"Yes. Of course." I grabbed the bag that held paper and pencils, ready for tedious note-taking. But at least it would be tedious note-taking somewhere different. "Shame to leave all this exciting filing work."

"Mmm. Well, I'll be sure to send more of it your way."

I froze, studying his face. Surely, he realized that I had spoken in jest. But Official Fredek's expression was blank. He was a hard one to read, but he was generally the nicer of all of the Officials. Now and then on my break he would let me wander the Atheneum, just to admire the sweeping walls of books and ladders, nearly disappearing far overhead. They said so much knowledge was contained in the Atheneum that, were one to read all it held, they would have the knowledge of a god.

The *wisdom* of a god, some said, but others said that was ridiculous. Knowledge does not give you wisdom.

No, wisdom takes a certain amount of common sense, which I had found lacking in most of the Charges. Magic could give you power, but it couldn't make you smart. Or kind. Or really even all that interesting.

A boy in the rich green robes of a Charge, with dark hair neatly tied back, waited for Official Fredek.

"Siya," Official Fredek said, pausing beside the boy. "This is Charge Semyon. He will be shadowing me today. Semyon, this is Siya Valdanova, one of our Clerks-in-training."

9

Semyon said nothing. He eyed me from shoes to hair, then sniffed. There was a deep crevice between his eyes; he was the picture of disdain. I dropped into a deep, slightly sarcastic curtsy.

He nodded approvingly, as though a curtsy was exactly what he would expect. My face boiled.

Official Fredek rubbed a hand over his hair, blond but flecked with grey, and then turned towards the door.

The morning was cool, with a light breeze that toyed about the streets. There was always a small breeze – though never wind. It gave a constant sense of movement. Of the city never being settled in one place. Like riding in a cart with your eyes closed, your hair dancing about a bit. Unsettled.

The sky was, as ever, a mottled, indescribable grey. Once blue, of course, before the city had been doomed to wander through nothingness, adrift on the waves of nowhere.

Perhaps I would be less sour if my days were punctuated with the sight of a clear blue sky and a shining sun. Or perhaps I would be this way anyway. There was really no way to know.

The crowds in the city streets parted to let us pass through, their eyes darting to Fredek's lavender robes, which denoted him as a Guild Official. I was dressed in grey and a bit of drab brown, and kept a careful distance, staying a few paces behind him and Semyon at all times.

The only evidence that I worked for the Guild was the small signet of a globe, which I kept in my pocket. I never had to show it. If ever I was out on Guild business, I was always with someone more important.

Our path led us past a street that offered a quick, passing view of the palace far across the city. Somewhere inside lived the queen, though no one had seen her in years. No one even knew if she was still alive.

I pulled my eyes away quickly.

"Official Fred," I started, intending to enquire about where the house in question was located, so that I could begin taking my notes, but Charge Semyon hissed at me over his shoulder, so sharply that I fell silent. He then began speaking to Fredek himself, a conversation which I couldn't quite hear.

I pulled a face at his back, and I began to sketch a rat on my paper as we made our way through the city. A rat with smoothed-back hair and a furrow between his eyes. I was just adding devilish horns to the rat on the paper when I bumped into the back of Official Fredek, who'd stopped walking.

"Something you want to share?" he asked, quizzically eyeing my sketch. We'd stopped by a house – presumably our destination.

"Oh, no," I said, letting my eyes wander up until they met Semyon's smouldering pools of misery. "I saw a very large rat. Never seen one so large, in fact. Fancied a sketch

11

while we walked. I like to document things, you know. It's why I excel at being a Clerk. Almost a Clerk, anyway."

"A rat could excel at being a Clerk. It requires no skill," Semyon said.

"I cannot allow talk like that, Charge Semyon," Fredek said disapprovingly. "Without our Clerks, we wouldn't survive. I ought to set you a week of notes and filing as punishment."

Semyon glared at me, and I smiled inside.

"I wasn't trying to insult anyone," he muttered.

"I was insulted." I wanted to offer a true smile at seeing him knocked down a peg or two, but I made sure to keep my face serious. To let them both know how deeply his words had cut me.

"We will deal with this later," Official Fredek said. "We mustn't keep the poor soul trapped down there much longer." He rapped four times on the door. A frantic woman with wild eyes and bird's nest hair opened it almost immediately.

"You're here," she gasped. "I thought you would never arrive. Come. This way. I'll show you where the door ought to be." She led us to a bare wall. "See? There should be a door here. But there isn't! I knew we should never have listened to that snivelling magical architect – he wasn't from the Guild, but his price was so reasonable, you know? Can you blame us?"

"Yes. Indeed I can," Official Fredek replied, eyeing the wall. "Magic is not something on which to skimp."

"Well, I think we've learned that now." The woman put both hands to her face. "Do you think he's all right? I've heard not a peep. Could he have suffocated? Or… Or starved to death?"

"How long has he been down there?"

"A few hours now."

"Then, no. I don't think so," Fredek replied calmly.

I made notes as quickly as I could, while Official Fredek felt around the wall. Semyon was careful to keep a solid distance between us, lest my *Clerkiness* should rub off on him.

I watched as he began to sketch out a map of the house on Guild parchment. That was what it was all about. Maps and magic and creation and mending. How unfair, that the parchment would never be in *my* hands. Only cheap note-taking paper, and an old pen.

I ducked my head and scribbled notes even less legibly than before.

When Official Fredek had thoroughly examined the wall, he took the parchment from Semyon. As their hands briefly touched the paper, a distinct crackle erupted, and watched longingly.

The Official held the parchment in both hands, pausing occasionally to run his fingertips along the wall where he wished the door to be, while speaking an enchantment at a low but consistent volume. The woman watched through her fingers, seemingly terrified of what might go wrong this time.

13

She needn't have worried. As far as magic went, her husband was in good hands. Official Fredek was who I would want fixing my troubles, if ever the need arose, which it certainly would not. I wasn't foolish enough to think magic could be bought cheaply.

As the seconds ticked by and Fredek carried on with his incantation, a shape began to materialize on the wall, little more than a shadow at first, but quickly deepening and transforming into a door with a small, round handle. A moment later, the sound of pounding started up from the other side. The woman opened the door with a shriek.

"Grigory!" she cried, clutching his face, lest he should disappear again. "Are you well? Are you well? You must be starving!" The man looked tired and frazzled, but entirely well otherwise.

"Yes. He is clearly quite well," Official Fredek said, with an edge of impatience. "And he shall eat. But first, we have some business."

I handed the man a citation I had filled out on the way, and finished with their address.

"This fine must be paid in full within the month. You can pay us a visit at the Guild to do so, but if we don't see you, we'll send someone around. And I suppose you can't remember the name of the fellow who landed you in this predicament?"

The woman shook her head.

"Not even a hint, I'm afraid," said the man.

Official Fredek snorted. It was the same lie that everyone gave. "No one ever can. Nevertheless, should you miraculously recall his name, do tell us, and it might result in a lower fine. Unauthorized magic is dangerous and foolhardy. The Guild exists for a reason. I do hope you will remember that in the future. Mishaps by magic dealers have led to far worse endings than this."

I shivered, remembering the stories of terrible misfortunes. With any luck, one of them would happen to Semyon one day.

"Be well." Official Fredek turned, and made for the front door with long strides. Semyon followed close on his heels, head held high and shoulders back. I trotted along behind them.

A few spectators had gathered outside to see what had come of the visit from the Guild Official. When we hurried past them, offering no clues or hints, they began to disperse with a grumble. Sometimes, when unauthorized magic resulted in something much bigger happening, it would draw a crowd large enough to fill the city streets. Like if a bridge disappeared, or an entire neighbourhood seemed to no longer exist – thrown into some invisible plane, but still retrievable by someone from the Guild. There was little else to interest or amuse, ever since we'd vanished from the real world, years before I was born. People needed *something* to distract themselves.

Semyon made a point of not casting a single glance my

way. I might have vanished from the world entirely and he would be none the wiser. To entertain myself as we walked, I made a game of pulling faces at the back of his head, holding my fingers behind him so it looked like he had devil's horns. Childish, but the walk was boring, through a part of the city I had been to a hundred times, with nothing new to see and nothing to hold my interest.

Until.

I found myself stopping suddenly beside an empty alleyway, as abruptly as if someone had called my name. It almost felt like they had. My hand still hung in the air with the fingers curled up like horns.

Semyon and Fredek carried on unaware, but I found myself staring down the alleyway. There was something there. A presence, maybe. A feeling of something lurking, or someone watching. Something sizzled in the air. It was unlike anything I had felt before, but it was how I had always imagined magic to feel.

But the alleyway was empty. Once again, my longing for adventure had let my mind run wild. So I turned and ran, catching up to Semyon and Official Fredek just as they were reaching the doors of the Guild once more.

"I appreciate your time, Siya," Official Fredek said, taking the parchment from Semyon and heading for the grand staircase that led into the mystical and elusive upper levels of the Guild.

I had been upstairs before, of course, on occasion. That

was where most of the business happened. I knew there was much more to explore, but it was only for those with magic – the headquarters of the Guild was like a puzzle that I would never get to finish.

"Feodor, how are you?" Semyon said, and my heart lurched. I whirled. He was reaching to shake the hand of a boy I had never properly met but felt as though I knew already, every inch of his face ingrained in my mind. A marvellously handsome, insufferable boy who knew nothing of my quiet little existence, and probably never would.

Feodor Sevastyen, the son of the man set to be the next Guild Elder. A boy, I had heard, with more map magic than a room full of Charges combined. He wore a long deep red coat that reached nearly to his knees, with carelessly fastened gold buttons.

Memories danced to life, even though I tried to squash them. All the years I had spent haunting the Guild while my father was working, watching the Charges come and go from their lessons – watching the way they too gazed upon Feodor with starry eyes, the jewel in the crown of the Guild. His name was on everyone's lips, his face in everyone's hearts – even mine.

I remembered all the nights I had spent falling into dreams of him after lying awake for hours, imagining conversations with him. What things he would say, and what things I would say. Finding new ways to sound intriguing and important. Ways to enchant the magical boy.

We would never have magic in common, so there had to be something else, something far more interesting, to keep his attention on me.

But those long nights of dreaming had ended. Eventually, I had grown up, and realized that the Guild was crawling with Charges and Officials just like Semyon. All cut from the same pompous cloth. All pretentious and self-righteous to the point of being insufferable. Feodor was probably the worst of them all.

"Ah..." said Feodor, clearly floundering for Semyon's name. Everyone liked to pretend that they knew Feodor. Even me, once upon a time.

"Semyon," said Semyon coldly. He recovered, and flashed a quick smile. "Just back from a house call. All fixed up. Easy-peasy."

Easy-peasy. Rat. I rolled my eyes. As if Semyon had done anything other than stand around, looking superior. It was Official Fredek who had performed the fix.

I pushed past them and made for the small room with my desk at a quick gait, lest my tongue should depart the stable just to see what trouble it could find.

"Do you have something to say?"

It was Feodor's voice. I stopped walking and turned, slowly. For the first time ever, Feodor was looking at me. On purpose.

"Are you speaking to me?" I asked, laying a hand delicately on my chest and arching an eyebrow in

18

exaggerated shock. My father would tell me to be respectful, but my father wasn't here, and I was in no mood to indulge another enchanter.

"Yes. I am."

I dropped into another ridiculous curtsy. "Your Grace, forgive me. Yes. I was rude." I had read in books that people often referred to royalty as *Your Grace*, even though it was never used in the Guild.

Such a notable person naturally deserved the utmost respect from everyone, and since he would forget about me the moment I left his line of sight, what did it matter if I was being ridiculous?

"Pay her no mind," Semyon said. "I've spent the last hour with her. Lost cause, if you know what I mean." He tapped his temples meaningfully.

I flushed and started forward, but Feodor spoke first, anger crackling across his face.

"Guild Charges shouldn't speak so of anyone. Do I need to report back to Official Fredek or my father on your character, Semyon? It would not be a good one. You know what I mean?" He took a single slow step towards Semyon, who in turn took a single slow step back, shaking his head.

"No."

"No?"

Semyon shook his head again.

"Are you not late for a class?"

Semyon swallowed and turned, trotting across the foyer like a scolded child.

I smiled as I watched him go, so small and pathetic and silly. So full of misplaced pride. Or maybe it *wasn't* misplaced; I didn't know enough about magic to tell whether he was gifted or not. I hoped he wasn't. I hoped he was as useless as I imagined he was.

Then I felt Feodor's eyes on me, and I stopped smiling. I cut my eyes towards him.

"I wish you hadn't spoken up," I said, more haughtily than I meant to. "I am well equipped to fend for myself. And it's boring enough around here, as it is. I was looking forward to a fight." I lightly punched one fist into the other hand.

"I'm not sure it would have been a fair one." Feodor's eyes smiled.

"I know. You're probably right. Imagine if I'd *killed* him!" I tossed my loose hair back over my shoulder, and headed to the stairs in search of my father.

But I did let myself glance back, just briefly – and found Feodor *smiling*.

Ugh. I was going for shocking. Besides, I didn't know enchanters had a sense of humour.

My father never liked being bothered in the middle of the day, but I was owed a short break after the house call, and a small part of me hoped that if I complained about Semyon enough, then maybe something would be done

20

about him. Maybe he would be reminded that my father was a Magister, and that I ought to be left alone.

That sounded a bit weak and pathetic, the more I thought about it, but someone really ought to humble him up a bit.

My father and the other Magisters – the highest-ranking map enchanters in the Guild, second only to the Elder – were usually to be found on the second floor, but I couldn't find them in their usual rooms. So I went back to the stairs to climb up to the next floor.

I used to see more of him. I would bring him a lunch from my mother every day at noon and we'd chat about whatever took my fancy that day. But that had all changed. Now I was lucky to catch a glimpse of him once during the whole day.

On the fourth floor, I finally heard voices emanating from a room down a hallway to the right. I rarely came up this far, unless I had mail to deliver. It wasn't that I was strictly forbidden from being up here, but it was definitely frowned upon.

My feet slowed as I approached the room, and a voice came from within.

"I need to take this back where it belongs, in the Sanctum."

"Discreetly, I hope. Stick it under your cloak, or in a book. A book always works. No one ever questions a book."

I slipped to the side of the door and carried on listening.

I knew I should announce my presence or walk away, but I didn't, because I was nosy and this sounded like something that I wanted to hear.

"Thank you for the advice." The speaker was deadpan. A bit sarcastic. "I'd never have thought of that on my own." I knew that voice. It was Official Fredek.

"You jest, Fredek, but if anyone finds out that we've got another piece…"

That voice was my father's. I frowned. *What piece? What was Fredek smuggling out to hide in the Sanctum?*

Before I had time to move, Official Fredek stepped out of the room, clutching a book, and shut the door behind him. He froze when he saw me, his hand still on the door handle.

"Siya. How long have you been there?"

I pushed off from the wall. "I just arrived. I came to see my father. Is he around?"

"He is." Something flickered in his eyes as he watched me. He opened the door again, and called, "Magister Davor, there's someone here for you." Then he moved past me and made for the stairs.

My father came to the door, his brow furrowed. A large table of Magisters and Officials flickered behind him for a moment, before he closed the door behind him. "Yes, Siya?" he said, exasperation tinging his voice. "What is it?"

His irritation took me aback. "I – I just came to say hello," I said, suddenly grasping for words. "I'm sorry. I ran into Semyon, one of the Charges, and I—"

"I'm busy right now, Siya," he told me. "I'll speak to you later, all right? Off you go." He moved his hand as though brushing something away, and then disappeared back into the room, shutting it firmly in my face.

I stood there staring at the door, feeling a bit like a cold breeze had swept through the hallway after he'd gone.

2

"I'm not feeling well today," I told my father in the morning. The lie tumbled out far too easily.

"You aren't well?" my father echoed, eyeing me up and down as he slipped on his ink-dark robes. Black robes. The symbol of a Guild Magister.

"Yes." I put the back of my hand to my forehead in a show of *unwellness*, thought it was perhaps too much, and blinked. "A headache. And my belly. And – no, that's all. Just those two things. But it's terribly unpleasant."

"You seemed quite well yesterday." He tucked a necklace I hadn't seen before beneath his robes. Like twine with a pendant that I couldn't quite see.

"I was. At least, I *thought* I was. Maybe I was a bit tired, come to think of it. One of the Charges seemed unwell and I think maybe he—"

"Very well. Stay and rest. I'll give your excuses to the Guild."

He walked briskly out. Usually I found his impatience to leave me – the only one of his three children born without a trace of magic – insulting, but today it came as a relief.

I stared at the wall where my father had just stood, his absent form almost a visible shadow against the wall. People like him would sometimes leave a slight impression in the space they left, like a freshly made bed that you'd lain on for a moment before standing up. I didn't know if this was magic or just the sheer force of his personality. That intangible quality people would call, reverently, a "presence".

I wasn't unwell, of course. I had simply decided not to go to work today. Instead, I was going to slip into the Atheneum, while Yarik, the librarian, took his morning nap. Sometimes – rarely – knowing so much useless information about the Guild paid off. I had spent so many years wandering around the Guild waiting for my father that I had collected lots of little secrets.

What precisely I planned to do at the Atheneum, I wasn't quite certain, but I couldn't face another day at the Guild, being sneered at by Semyon and ignored by everyone else. Filing papers and filling out ledgers and alphabetizing citations.

It was all just too much. I needed a chance to breathe.

To get away from the Semyons of the Guild and remember what I loved about working there. And, like I said, I was nosy. The fleeting mention of the Sanctum, hidden beneath the Atheneum, that sense that Fredek had been hiding something down there, had steeped in my mind throughout the night until I couldn't ignore it any longer. So I was going to visit the Atheneum, and the Sanctum, and poke around in places I shouldn't, just because I could.

Magic or no magic, *I* could get into the Sanctum. Something no one else could do.

I made a show of feeling unwell as I helped my mother wrangle my brother and sister, Stepan and Sara. Sara was the youngest of us three, at only eight, while Stepan sat in the middle, at twelve. There was always a contented tiredness in my mother's eyes, mornings spent readying them for school, days spent baking for a nearby bakery, forever ignoring the magic that slept quietly under her skin.

I couldn't quite imagine having it and not wanting it. But, although she was technically a member of the Guild, she found it infrequently useful, and a part of her life that just didn't quite belong.

Imagine.

I would watch her sometimes when she wasn't looking, freckled cheeks, hair in disarray, content in her gentle, magicless life, and I would wonder how it could be so.

After my brother and sister had left for school – regular old school, still too young to learn how to use magic properly at the Guild – and my mother had left for the bakery, I tied on my cloak and slipped out of the house. The path that led to the street was full of brown grass that sometimes hinted at being green. Back when the city was part of Sarsova, it had probably been a lush garden, overflowing with flowers and bushes. Now it was just another reminder of what we had lost.

I cracked my knuckles nervously as I slipped along the street, head down. The last thing I needed was some random Official out on an errand to recognize me.

Crack. I passed a cart selling questionable concoctions that the seller claimed cured headaches. *Crack*. A young couple laughed and held hands as they walked far too slowly along the street. I darted around them. *Crack*. A child chased a wooden ball into the street and nearly tripped me up.

What exactly is your plan for today, Siya? a little voice in my head queried.

Truthfully, I didn't know.

When I was younger, I used to love exploring the Guild building. Sneaking through the shadows and hiding in corners. Mostly in the Atheneum, because in the library were a hundred thousand ideas and worlds I wanted to be a part of. Lives far more interesting than mine. It had grown to be my favourite place. I had made it mine.

Having a Magister for a father meant that I had endless hours to fill as he worked. But then he had decided that

I should learn to be a Clerk, and the Guild became less of a playground and more of a cage.

Shard was bustling as I traipsed along the streets. Carts rumbled by, and more than once, I had to press myself up against a building to keep out of the way. The smell of dishwater sometimes collided with the scent of baking, steam curling through an open window. Stone buildings sometimes broke up to reveal thready alleyways barely as wide as my shoulders.

I kept the hood of my cloak up to hide my face. I felt safe in the disguise. Safe hidden in the shadows of the fabric.

One would think having a Magister for a father, as I did, would mean I would know something of their business, but that wasn't the case. My father rarely spoke a word to any of us about his work. Sometimes over dinner, when he was around for it, he would mention a joke, or something interesting he had heard, but it always ended there. He was too important to share his work at the table.

Finally, the Guild loomed before me. A massive building, large enough to house all the classrooms, meeting rooms, the Atheneum, and the Sanctum, running deep underground. It was a castle, technically, but I had never thought of it that way. It wasn't quite pretty enough to earn that title. Not like the ones I had read about in storybooks.

This was risky, playing sick and then sneaking right

back into the place where I was meant to be working, but after so much boredom, the risk brought on a real thrill.

I knew there was a small door that led into the main foyer that was often left unlocked during the day. I watched it for a few long moments as the city whirled around me, and when no one had come or gone for several long minutes, I darted forward.

Inside, it was mostly quiet. A few Charges walked in a group and chatted amongst themselves. A Clerk walked past, carrying a copy of the Shard city code. The large desk where visitors were meant to check in sat unmanned, thankfully. A quiet morning. Just what I needed.

I walked casually across the foyer. If I was good at doing anything, it was being boringly normal. I walked to the grand staircase with the stride of someone who was running an errand and couldn't be interrupted. The staircase split. I paused to listen for footsteps rising up from below, but, hearing nothing, I began descending the right set of stairs. An ornate gold railing slid smoothly under my palm, trailing away into the lower levels of the Guild. At the end of each banister was a globe, carved with a map of the city.

"...and I would have thought little of it, other than..."

My father. Panic thundered through me. Why did he have to be right here, right now?

I turned and fled back up the steps. I hurried to the stairwell on the opposite side, trying to keep my steps quiet, and took it so quickly I nearly tumbled the whole way down.

I knew he would be here, of course, but why couldn't he be hiding upstairs like he so often did?

When I stopped near the bottom to listen, I could hear my father's voice carrying away, off into the foyer and fading.

No one else was around.

I took a moment to gather myself after the near-miss with my father. Perhaps he wouldn't have cared very much, but he certainly would have had questions about my presence here today after I'd told him I was unwell this morning.

I slipped down the rest of the stairs. Before me stood the great doors of the Atheneum, in the shape of two great books standing side by side. Spines towards me. An inscription across the doors read: *In knowledge lies everything. In everything, there is magic.*

The words always made me shiver, even though I'd read them a hundred times. Their grandeur. Their weight.

Behind those doors lay seemingly endless tomes and words. Nearly boundless possibilities, bound only by time. One could never read everything in a short human lifespan.

Cautiously, I poked my head inside the doors and eyed Yarik. Asleep. He never failed to take that mid-morning nap. I couldn't help but smile. Everyone loved Yarik. Warm. Friendly. Known for reading long past his bedtime and making up for it during work hours.

On silent feet, I went through a cracked-open door and

padded softly across the library's foyer until pillars hid me from sight. I was standing in the circular Atheneum. A rich green rug yawned across the expanse before me. Shelves upon shelves, ladders as slender and fine as spiders' webs clinging to the walls of books, a ceiling painted to resemble the starry night sky we never got to see.

A thread of a moon peeked out from some painted black treetops, far across the room, rising to watch over the Atheneum.

I loved to stand here and stare at the so-called sky. Imagine what it would be like to see the real stars, the real midnight-blue canopy enshrouding the great beyond. Feel the cool winter breeze as the stars gleamed above, so close and so far. Dream about the world that was still out there, hidden by magic.

All those years I had spent waiting around for my father, or following him to work when he didn't know it, had mostly seen me lurking here, amongst the books. I was never looking for anything specific, just wandering the shelves, picking up books to read. Books about old kings and queens, tales from the hills below the mountains, books about the most beautiful gardens in Sarsova. Books about all the things I hoped to see if we were ever reunited with the rest of Sarsova. Never anything about magic, if I could help it.

This Atheneum had been my playground, and now it felt like walking back through the doors of my childhood.

I felt my heart lift. Maybe *this* was why I'd come here today. To be around the kind of magic that *I* could feel. Could cherish the way others cherished real magic.

Books.

Books never made me feel ashamed, the way others in the Guild did. They didn't care who or what I was. They imparted their magic to me all the same.

Behind me, Yarik stirred in his sleep, and I hurried out of his sight. I thought I heard the great doors open and close, and I quickly let the shadows swallow me, in among the smaller shelves where the lights didn't reach as well. Lanterns were lit every day either by hand or by magic. I was never quite sure which. They led to a sort of back hallway that wound behind the tallest walls of books, with outlets now and then to pop out and back into the central part of the library.

I peered back towards Yarik, but he was long out of sight behind pillars and books and reading desks. Satisfied, I was about to carry on, when I was *almost* certain I saw the tip of a shoulder momentarily protrude from behind a shelf before again disappearing.

You are not the only one allowed in the Atheneum, I reminded myself, though my heart raced. *Even if you wish you could be.*

I let a hand trail over the backs of the books as I moved towards a very tall ladder against a giant wall of old literature.

The ladder itself was coated in dust. Though it appeared to be on rails like the others, this one couldn't move. It wasn't just any ladder. After turning in a full circle to ensure no one was around, I reached behind a nearby book. *Earliest Sarsovan Settlements*. A large, cloth-bound volume that bore illustrations on nearly every page. But I wasn't there for the book. Rather, for what I had hidden behind it.

A cold, hard thing rested on the shelf behind, squeezed between the book and the wall: a key. I slipped the key into the gold filigree on the spine of another book.

This was magic, or as close as I could get. A secret door, made to blend in with the rest of the library, only opened through map magic – or so they thought.

No one had noticed the keyhole in the secret door – why would they, when they didn't need to use it? But I had noticed it. And I had gone off on a grand treasure hunt for the key that went with it. Another way of playing as I explored the Atheneum. Another cherished memory of this place.

Eventually, after months of scouring every inch of the place, I had found it tucked away in the back of a closet, gathering dust in amongst a box of keys of all shapes and sizes. Discarded as useless by those who didn't need to bother with such non-magical items any more.

Magic was everything, they said. But a good, old-fashioned key worked too, and, somewhere along the line, they had forgotten that. I hugged the thought to myself.

The lock clicked. The secret door cracked open.

I shivered, smiling, and stepped through the door that led to the Sanctum.

A narrow passageway greeted me just beyond the spectral books, which carried on for a few yards before ending at a winding staircase wrapped tightly around a pole. The stairs were cramped and unnerving, barely more than a bit of iron coiled around the pole that seemed to sink deep into the ground. I spiralled down, one step at a time, until the staircase ended.

My legs unsteady from the careful descent, I stood still, breathing, listening. Were those footsteps, or phantoms born of my fear of being followed?

After a moment of listening to the silence, I adjusted my cloak and stepped forward. I was in a wide but low hallway, with rooms branching off that were too dark to see in properly. If the Atheneum was the lifeblood of the Guild, then the Sanctum was the heart. The beating, pulsing core, filled with the richest, darkest secrets. The things most knew nothing about. Rooms that bore no lock, no key, leaving their safety to the only thing the Guild trusted completely: map magic. There were pathways that must be followed exactly, stones that must be touched, doors approached in just the right way. It could take decades for someone to work it out on their own.

I couldn't work the magic and find all the secrets, but I could still find the Sanctum, and that felt like something.

The space opened up, the hall now only marked by tall stone pillars as old as the ground itself. Large archways led into various stone rooms. The air had gone from feeling old to ancient, every breath in my lungs a rush of history.

I stopped. Ahead, outside one of the stone rooms, stood a guard. In his hand was an elegant, deadly sharp spear, glistening in the faint candlelight. He didn't move, seemed hardly to breathe, only stared straight ahead, silent, guarding.

Seconds ticked by.

I had never seen a guard down here before, in all the times I had sneaked around. What was he guarding?

The guard still hadn't moved. Standing taller and taking a deep breath, I stepped forward.

He didn't move. He didn't blink. And if I looked closely enough, he *didn't* breathe. An illusion. I let out a small laugh.

"Did he make a joke?"

Coldness and fear made my skin tingle. Swallowing, I turned to find Feodor Sevastyen in the hallway behind me.

He wore the same long red coat with the gold buttons. His hands hung at his sides. A mess of short dark waves framed strong and graceful features. He wasn't smiling, but he didn't look angry either.

"You shouldn't sneak up on people. It's impolite, you know." I shook off my fright, willing my limbs to stop shaking. Would he tell on me? What would my father say?

"And probably you shouldn't be skulking through the Sanctum, where none of us are allowed without a Magister."

I stood taller. "And *quite* probably you should mind your own business." Daring words.

"Oh. Ouch." He winced a little, his face twitching with what looked dangerously close to a smile. "He isn't real, I presume?" He nodded to the guard.

"No." I swept my hand through the guard's midriff, meeting only air. "I knew he wasn't."

"Did you? You seemed very nervous."

"That's because I thought I was being followed."

"You were being followed."

"I know that now, of course," I said. "How can they map a *person*?"

"With great difficulty," Feodor replied. "He isn't really a person. Just a phantom, designed by magic. He's meant to scare people off, before they get close enough to realize that he isn't real."

I cut the guard a sharp look, and then turned back to Feodor. "Why were you following me? Am I so terribly interesting?" I swept a hand dramatically through my hair.

I saw him bite back a definite smile. Who would have thought that the high and mighty Feodor would have a sense of humour?

"Yes," he said. "I wanted to know what brought you to the Sanctum, against the rules. That *is* very interesting.

Even with my father being who he is, I'm not sure I'll be able to talk us out of this one." There was a hint of excitement in his voice, as though this was exactly the kind of trouble he had been looking for.

"This isn't an *us* situation," I told him, even though the word *us* made me feel something I very quickly stomped down on. *He is basically Semyon, with another name,* I reminded myself. Better-looking, maybe, but still the same. "I don't need you to talk me out of anything. Now, if you don't mind, could you please leave me alone? I don't need any meddling magical people following me around. I'm not here to do anything bad."

Feodor took one step closer, and my chest tightened. "So, what are you here to do?"

I looked away from him, just briefly, to collect my wild thoughts. Too many different feelings jostled for attention. A touch of embarrassment at getting caught. A spot of anger that it had to be Feodor, of all people. Confusion that he was so unexpectedly easy to talk to.

"My personal affairs are none of your concern," I said in the end. "It's impolite to ask."

"And you care a great deal about being polite."

"I do."

"How did you get down here?"

"Magic." I raised my eyebrows in quick succession, mysteriously.

His eyes narrowed thoughtfully. "I don't mean to cause

offence, but I think we established your … magicless-ness yesterday."

I bristled. "I didn't say it was *my* magic. Here, if you must know." I held up the key I had slipped into my pocket. "Just a standard key, for a magical door. Sometimes, even ordinary people like me can find their way into extraordinary places."

"You don't seem ordinary to me. How did you know there was a key?"

"I know lots of things." I said it with a wink that was perhaps a bit too much. *He didn't think I was ordinary*, I thought.

He rubbed his forehead and sighed. "Fine. If you won't tell me what you want to do down here, then at least let me do it with you."

"I'm … accustomed to being alone."

"So, be alone no more," he said, with a twinkle. "Let me keep you company."

I didn't want his company.

I was almost entirely sure about that.

Almost.

"I…" My voice trailed off. I found myself staring at him, remembering all the whispers I'd heard from the Charges and Clerks, about how much magic he carried, how he might one day run the Guild. Strange to be so close to him, seeing him breathe and blink and eye me with an expression I couldn't place. Someone so revered, barely an arm's length away.

I told myself to grow up. This was just another part of Feodor's magic: the spell he cast over everyone. Sooner or later, all grew to love him. I, for one, would not be taken in. Absolutely not.

I didn't have to get to know him to learn he was just like Semyon. They were all the same, in the end. I had met enough Charges to know that.

"Come on," he said, his eyes still on my face. "This way, we can get into trouble together."

"I doubt very much that you'd get into as much trouble as me." The son of the man who would be the next Guild Elder? Honestly. A slap on the wrist, at the worst. Most likely, no one would even bat an eyelid. He could go where he wanted. Do what he wanted.

"Oh?" He let out a whispered laugh. "Shall we find out?"

Bumps rose along my arms. I could leave right now, find my way back up the winding staircase, slip back through the Atheneum, and return home, where Father thought I was right now. That was what a reasonable person would do.

But I have been feeling so very unreasonable.

Or I could stay here, carry on through the Sanctum, keep breaking the rules, and see what trouble I could get into with Feodor Sevastyen.

The choice was clear. I stepped past Feodor, and into the very heart of the Sanctum.

3

"What are we looking for?"

Feodor walked close to me, but not so close as to make me uncomfortable. Just the right amount of closeness.

We passed small, dusty rooms. I felt completely distracted by his presence. "Oh, just … you know. Things. Something I want to find."

"That's very specific. I'll be sure to keep an eye out for *things*."

I flushed. I wasn't sure whether I could trust him with what I had heard outside the Magisters' meeting room and Fredek's furtive demeanour.

If I told him, he might tell someone else, and soon everyone would be laughing at magicless Siya, who overheard a scrap of conversation and jumped to ridiculous conclusions. Which I had done. Did I really think that a piece of *the* map might be hidden here? The one that would reunite Shard with the rest of Sarsova? And did I really believe that I was going to be the person to find it?

On the other hand … maybe he would find it interesting and help me search. Maybe I *could* get him into trouble.

I tried to buy myself some time. "I thought there must be something important down here. Why else would this place exist?"

Feodor's steps slowed briefly and I could feel his eyes on me. "Siya? Do you – may I call you Siya?"

"It would be strange if you didn't," I said drily. "Given that it's my name."

"Right. Of course. Um – Siya? Do you *know* something important is down here?"

I couldn't meet his gaze, so I carried on walking, concentrating far too hard on my footsteps. "I don't know what you're talking about."

"I think you do. I think you're looking for something specific. Something you heard is down here."

"That doesn't sound like me. I'm not even a Clerk yet. What could I possibly have heard?" I looked at him with wide, innocent eyes.

Feodor snorted. "I hardly know you, but I think it *does* sound like you."

"Rude. You're implying I'm a busybody who goes poking around off-limits places, looking for things I shouldn't. I think you owe me an apology." The words came out so

41

easily because they were exactly, one hundred per cent the truth.

"I am so, so sorry that I am right about you and your intentions. This must be really difficult for you." He put a hand on his heart and raised his eyebrows like he was in earnest.

I fought off a smile. "If I tell you, you might not believe me, or you might get into trouble. I'm a bad influence that way."

"I'm in the market for some trouble. It's all a bit boring up there." His eyes flicked up towards the Guild overhead.

I bit the inside of my cheek, thinking. "I think there's something down here. Something very important."

"See? I was right. But that's why this place exists. To keep things safe."

"Or to keep Shard safe from the things down here," I said.

"Now *that's* interesting."

I felt a bit like I was dangling on the edge of a cliff. It was frightening to let go, but it was tempting too. To fall, to let him into my secret and see what he thought of it.

I stepped closer to Feodor so that I could whisper. He tilted his head down to look me in the eyes. "I think the Guild has the map," I said quietly. "Or some of it, at least. A piece other than the one in the frame."

I waited for the laughter, because certainly, to him, the idea would be ridiculous. I lifted my chin a bit higher, so he would know that I was ready for it.

Feodor was quiet for a long moment, and I shifted uncomfortably. Any second now.

"Why do you think that?"

I cleared my throat. *If anyone finds out we have another piece...* "I overheard something yesterday, outside where the Magisters were meeting. About a *piece* of something, to be brought down here."

Feodor stared at me for a long moment. "I don't know what I was expecting you to say, but that wasn't it."

I stepped back a bit. "I told you I was trouble."

He nodded. "That's a lot of trouble," he said absently. He was frowning. "I'm fairly certain you weren't meant to have heard that. And I'm not sure..."

"Not sure of what?"

"Not sure why the Guild would have another one of the three missing pieces."

I shrugged. I had been prepared for laughter, but not that he might take it quite so seriously. "Any number of reasons, probably. To keep it safe until they can find the final one, maybe. I'm going to ask my father, once I'm sure it's here."

"I'm sure *that* will go well." He flicked his eyebrows up briefly. Sarcastically.

"It will be worth getting into trouble to get the answers."

"I suppose so." He nodded again, slowly, thoughtfully.

I looked around. Small stone rooms branched off the hallway, seeming to carry on for ever. "There are too many

43

rooms down here. I doubt I'll ever find it, anyway."

"You haven't been looking in the right places." There was an edge to his voice. A bit of humour I didn't understand.

I frowned, blinking a few times. "It's very frustrating when you speak in riddles, you know. I don't have all day."

With another hint of a smile, Feodor reached into his pocket and withdrew an old parchment, on which was drawn a map I had never seen before. Not that that was surprising. There were thousands of maps lurking about the Guild.

"You found the key to the Sanctum, yes. Very impressive, I grant you. But I have something else here." He tapped a knuckle on the parchment a few times. "What is the Sanctum? A series of rooms below the Guild, right? Most people don't get this far, so I have to commend you. But the things they hide down here are too precious to be trusted to only one layer of map magic. The books you walked through, the illusion of him" – he nodded back towards the guard – "those are all the first layers. But the Guild is the Guild. They will protect themselves, protect their magic, and protect their secrets, using the only thing they trust."

"More magic." Another piece of the puzzle I had known nothing about. More parts of the world hidden from me. I suppressed a frustrated sigh.

He nodded, a wistful look lingering on his face as he searched my eyes for something.

"How did you get that map?" I whispered. Suddenly

I worried that even the walls had ears.

"I told you, I like to get into trouble. I have had a lot of time to kill over the years, hanging around and waiting for my father. I figured out how to make my own map that could show me the secrets hidden away down here."

I drew in a long breath. Familiarity toyed with my heart. I too had spent time here waiting for my father. That was how I had come to know this place so well. How I had come to find the key. I knew what that kind of loneliness was like. Lurking. Wanting to belong. Trailing after a father who was far too busy to remember I was even here.

The only difference, really, was that Feodor did belong, in the end. I never did.

I tucked the thoughts away to go over later, and I looked down at the map in his hands. Then around at the stone hallway.

"Well," he said, holding out the map. "Would you like to see the real Sanctum?"

The real Sanctum. Suddenly, me finding the key to sneak down here didn't feel so special.

"If you don't mind." I said it coolly, not wanting him to know just thrilling I found this, or how disappointing my own secrets now seemed, in comparison.

My heart thundered. I shivered. People like me – the magicless – didn't often have moments like these, exploring hidden, magical parts of the city that were never meant for prying eyes. Nerves shook me, but it sure did beat sitting in the dusty office all day. Anything just to feel something.

Feodor placed both hands on the parchment, then began to speak, his voice low and rhythmic. The incantation poured out of him like a song I had been waiting to hear. Every word, each inflection, grew more bewitching and intoxicating. When he stopped, the silence felt like a shock.

My breath caught. I gazed around at the Sanctum, and I gently reached for the stone wall. Feodor looked up at me in silence, then around us. It was hardly the same place we had stood in moments before. The grim stone and endless, empty rooms had been replaced by well-lit, tidy rooms covered in red carpets, with ornate gold sconces lining the walls. Where each room had been empty, they now held innumerable articles, too many to place at a single glance. Wooden shelves held books and maps and quills, curiosities and star charts and figurines of the First Enchanters – the original mappers. The gods.

"What is this?" I whispered.

"This is magic," said Feodor quietly. "What do you think of it?"

"I don't know. I don't know what to think." I might never have known about such a place. Many like me never would. Beautiful secrets kept for magical eyes to see.

He let out a small laugh. "It is something to behold, indeed. The true Sanctum. Now shall we have a look around for this mysterious piece of map you heard about?"

I glanced behind us. "Aren't you worried someone will come in?"

"It's unlikely," he answered. "The Magisters are all in a meeting with my father upstairs, and most of the Officials are on their morning house calls. It's just you and me."

"Oh." I moved down the hall, pausing to look in each doorway I passed. "We won't find it in all this mess. Like a single cobblestone in a city of stone. It will never happen."

"Not with that attitude," Feodor said, turning to face me but walking backwards. "Have some heart. I have a good feeling about this. We'll find it."

I trailed behind him, careful not to get too close, though I wasn't sure why. Did I fear that my lack of magic would transfer to him? Or that a touch from him would singe my skin?

How proud I'd been about my stolen key, once upon a time. This new Sanctum, this peeling away layers of magic to show what lay hidden beneath, was, as always, far more interesting and beautiful than anything the unmagical world could create. And, once again, I felt very small as we wandered slowly down the hall.

We passed a cove of shelves built into the wall, full of wide-topped glass jars that held rolled-up maps. But not parchment maps, like were usually found around the Guild. Not magical maps. Just regular relic maps on old-fashioned paper. Maps like those before us used.

Maps people like me still used, because they were the only kind that got us anywhere.

Feodor hung close to my shoulder while I plucked the

largest one from a jar and carefully unrolled it. It had been coiled for so long it didn't want to unroll, so he held the two right corners of it for me. And before us unfurled a sprawling, wondrous map. Sarsova – the land beyond the wandering city. Our one true home, to which we would one day return.

I had studied maps of it before, but they were always smaller and less detailed, kept in the city library or hanging on the wall of a wealthy citizen that I would pore over while on a house call. But this one was different. The aged brown paper bore beautiful scrawls in an elegant hand, forming tiny trees to make up great forests, small houses with curling chimney smoke where a village sat, or a sprawling stone city made of hundreds of minuscule stones where Tryvinski, Sarsova's capital, stood, tall and proud. Shard was the capital of magic, but I had always heard that Tryvinski was far more grand. Sweeping and filled with spires and windows and secrets tucked away.

And then there was the north, where a thousand detailed mountain peaks made up the Bleaks, the largest, wildest mountain range in Sarsova. It was there that, long ago, most of the dreygas – magic-eating creatures that were somehow both human and not – had been sent, and kept there through map magic. Protecting Sarsova from their bloodthirsty ways. They could never leave the Bleaks, so long as the magic was kept intact, so if you never went there yourself, there was nothing to fear. The dreygas that had been left hiding in the city slowly disappeared, one by one. The Guild was said to have hunted them down, perhaps hoping that once they were all gone, Baba Yaga might free the city from its curse.

She never did.

My skin prickled with want. This map was a reminder of how rich and alive the world beyond was. How much life and death and beauty sat waiting for us to return. It hung in my dreams, that want. That need, to escape the confines of Shard and wander free and wild through a land that seemed never to end.

"One day." Feodor whispered the words beside me.

He was wrong. Sarsova had never been further away. I took the map away from him and rolled it up.

We wandered on.

I passed a room that was full of books piled atop a table. As though maybe they hadn't quite gotten around to organizing this room yet.

I walked past, then stopped and backed up. The memory of seeing Official Fredek carrying a book came back.

"Hmm," I said, and Feodor's head turned in my direction. "A whole room, just for books."

With Feodor only a few steps behind me, I entered the room and approached the table. The title of one of the books, in faded, barely legible words, was *The Days of Fedir and Brana: The First Enchanters*. It was a book nearly every member of the Guild had read at one point or another.

Something about it rang out as familiar, and not because I had seen it a hundred times before.

"Are you in the mood for something to read?" Feodor asked me after a moment. "Because, if so, I can recommend something far less likely to put you to sleep."

"Thank you, but my stack of books to read is bigger than your ego," I replied, as we both stood on opposite sides of the table. He flashed a quick smile at my words, and then looked down at the book again.

"Then what?" he asked.

"I don't know."

I gently picked up the book. The spine creaked with age, the pages so old they threatened to tumble to the floor. I flipped through a few of them, wondering if the cover was misleading and there was something else inside, but no. It was the same old story of Fedir and Brana that I had heard a hundred times before.

I set the book back on the table, then froze. A scrap of paper fluttered to the floor.

Our breath caught in the silent room, and for a moment, neither of us moved. It couldn't be ... could it? In the small piece of paper lying on the floor, I saw everything. The history of the city, the story I had heard so many times I could recite it in my sleep. The story of how the map enchantress Baba Yaga had bound the City of Shard's soul to a map and torn it into three pieces, to be blown away by the wind.

No one knew where the pieces were. Or so we thought.

Rumours surfaced all the time – a curious scrap of paper here, a sighting there – but the Guild had investigated each and every one of them, and found nothing of promise. Except, apparently, for this one. And the one in the frame.

I bent down slowly and picked up the scrap of paper. It was old. So old that I worried it would fall to pieces in my fingers. The paper bore bits of lines and scrawls, definitely part of a map, and definitely of the city.

Why in a book? Why not locked up somewhere safe? I wondered. Perhaps that would draw too much attention to it. Perhaps they felt that it was safer tucked away into the hidden, magical Sanctum, concealed in plain sight amongst the other million things that collected dust down here. Innocuous.

"Could it ... be?" I gingerly handed the paper over to Feodor, who took it carefully, as though it might sting him. I had wanted to find it, sure. Even allowed myself to hope. But the past half hour had felt more like a game than something real. Like two young kids skulking around behind their parents' backs, looking for hidden treasure in places they shouldn't. But now, it was real.

Feodor turned it over a few times, wordlessly. I imagined what he would say next. *We shouldn't be here,* he would say, in a serious Magister kind of voice. *Games are for children. The Guild keeps this place hidden for a reason.*

"It's magical, that's for sure," he said softly, running his fingertips over the surface.

"Just say it," I finally whispered. He looked up at me, his expression hard to read. "Go on."

"Say what?"

"That we aren't meant to be here. That I made a mistake and this is an ordinary piece of an ordinary map."

He looked back down at the piece of paper resting in his hands. Under his breath, he muttered a few incantations. It felt like an eternity passed while I waited.

"I don't think it was a mistake," he said at last. "I think this is a part of the map that Baba Yaga used to separate Shard from the rest of the world. Look. It matches the one in the frame, up in the foyer." He held it up and pointed to some faded lines and markings. I recognized them too. That map in the frame was as familiar to me as my own palm.

I looked from the map, to him, then back to the map. "Are you certain?"

"I'm … I'm fairly certain. The magic is very old. Very strong. Not like anything we use around here. It's … different."

My heart thundered, excitement and pride and maybe a little fear all flaring to life. Then I smiled. Adventure was appearing just before me, at long last.

My heart carried on thundering as we made our way back through the Sanctum and towards the winding stairs, the piece of the map tucked carefully into Feodor's coat pocket. The thick scent of dust and old stone closed in, and the air felt suddenly too heavy to breathe. Thoughts tumbled through my mind.

How have we not heard before that the Guild has found another part of the map?

Why are they keeping it a secret?

What will my father say when I tell him I found it?

We were nearly back at the stairs when I stopped, a noise pulling my attention away from my wild thoughts. In this new version of the Sanctum that Feodor had revealed, an arched stone doorway led into another hallway, and distantly, I saw what looked like cells.

"Siya?" Feodor said. "What is it?" He too peered into the hallway, to see what had drawn my attention away.

From deep within came another sound, much louder than before. A sound I couldn't fathom, couldn't place, but that sank right through my skin and rattled my bones. A voice – a scream – a laugh. All at once. Hollow – guttural – insidious. The few seconds the noise rang out stretched and warped into an eternity.

Beside me, Feodor had frozen, terror and confusion distorting his face.

"We should go," he said. "Now."

We left the Sanctum, and I climbed up the never-ending staircase so quickly my legs gave out and I arrived at the top of the stairs by crashing in a heap in the Atheneum.

It was largely empty, thankfully. In the light and normality of the Atheneum, what we had seen and heard seemed impossible. Had we imagined that sound, that scrap of ancient map?

No. I knew better than that.

We didn't speak as we climbed the stairs in search of our fathers. We weren't even certain where they would be, but they were always above stairs, sequestered in a room, doing very important business behind closed doors. Whatever that business was, somehow the Guild always ran smoothly, and classes were always taught seamlessly.

I glanced subtly at Feodor a few times, trying to read what thoughts were on his mind, but his face gave very little away.

After a breathless climb, a closed door greeted us on the third floor, hung with a sign that politely read: *Knock, please.*

We paused outside, gathering in a breath. I wondered for a minute what I would say, then I stopped trying to work it out and pushed open the door so hard it clattered against the wall.

My eyes took in the scene in the few seconds before they had registered our entrance. A large globe sat hovering above the table, both there and not. Visible and invisible, as though they were partway through an enchantment. I could see through it to the wall and the faces behind it, but its shape and lines were still there. A parchment lay on the table before my father and Ermolai, Feodor's father, and a handful of other Magisters, their fingers still resting on the incantations written there, their eyes lifting in sudden confusion and—

Fear.

Then everyone moved at once.

My father shoved his chair back so suddenly it fell to the floor behind him. Ermolai rolled up the parchment in a hurry, as the others in the room stood to form a makeshift wall that blocked the table.

"What do you think you're doing?" my father thundered, pushing us back out of the room by our shoulders and closing the door behind him, Ermolai close behind.

"We—" I choked as I tried to form the words and cleared my throat. "We had a question," I said.

"Did you not read the sign?" he snapped, waving a hand to the sign that hung on the door.

"We *did* knock," I lied. "You just didn't hear us."

"I doubt that."

"And you," Ermolai said to Feodor. "You truly ought to know better." The disappointment was heavy in his voice. I had never heard anyone address Feodor like that.

"I'm sorry," Feodor said simply, but he didn't sound remorseful. I watched him carefully tuck the piece of the map into his pocket, out of sight. "It won't happen again."

He didn't have to look at me, but I understood. The map was our secret now. Something to hide. My father

55

placed a hand on my shoulder and ushered me down the hall towards the stairs. I turned to look back at Feodor and his eyes met mine. *Our secret*, he was telling me, as his own father held him back for a private word.

He didn't have to tell me. Everything about the Guild had shifted in some indiscernible way, and a coldness crept into my body from where my father's hand gripped my shoulder.

4

The next day I awoke earlier than usual, and I decided to go into the Guild. Staying at home meant time to think, and right now, thinking was best avoided.

I had spent all night thinking. Of Feodor, so close to me. The scrap of parchment. That terrifying noise in the dungeon. And our fathers' faces as the door had slammed open.

After so long of nothing happening, now it felt like everything was.

As I trudged to work, I wrapped myself tightly in my cloak and kept my head down, feeling as though everyone in the city knew of my journey into the Sanctum yesterday. I glanced up at the hazy, blurry nothingness sky above the city, and wondered what my father would say when he saw me. I had walked into a secret, another one, in that room.

The Guild had secrets, certainly, as did everyone, but their sudden and vehement reaction felt like more than that. More than the kinds of secrets I was used to.

I wished someone could write me a map to take me back to a few days ago, when everything had been simpler. But at the same time, I had spent so long wishing for change that I knew I should accept it. Be grateful for it.

That was easier said than done.

I shivered again. I had shivered every time I remembered the noise we had heard. Threads seemed to be coming loose all around me. Questions rising at every corner.

My head throbbed like it had never done before.

The look in Feodor's eyes as we had paused outside those dungeons. The sound of his voice. It had made my blood run cold, and I couldn't shake the memory of it. And then I had seen a glimpse of it again, though smaller, when our fathers had come rushing from the meeting room. I thought of Feodor and the look on his face in that little room, holding the map. The boy who was always on top of the magical world, suddenly realizing just how much was kept even from him. The part of me that thought he was a bit high and mighty felt a pinch of satisfaction that he had been brought down to my level.

"Ah, Siya, just the person I want to see." Official Fredek

greeted me before the door to the Guild had even closed behind me. Behind him stood a group of five or six Charges, including Semyon.

"Oh?" I said, trembling a little. Did Fredek know what lay below our feet? What thing made that noise in the Sanctum?

"Indeed. Today, a number of Charges are off on an outing. You know the type. To mingle and get to know each other. I'd love for you to go and take notes." He leaned towards me, and spoke more quietly. "Tell me how they get on, see if there are any promising up-and-comers. That sort of thing. And then report back to me."

"When you say you'd love for me to go…" I started, eyeing the Charges unhappily. I'd gone on one before, while shadowing one of the actual Clerks, but this would be the first time I'd gone myself.

"I very much mean that is what you should do," Official Fredek replied with a cheerful and satisfied smile.

"If you're sure you can spare me," I said, sighing.

"Very sure," said Official Fredek. "You'll have fun. Get to know them a bit. Oh, and Feodor will be joining you! He is today's outing leader."

As he said it, Feodor came down the stairs from one of the upper levels, looking remarkably calm and refreshed given what had happened yesterday. His eyes caught mine only for a second, as they would catch the gaze of someone he had never properly met.

Had yesterday even happened? Or were things as they always had been?

I sighed loudly enough for Fredek to hear, then I marched past them all to my tiny office, grabbed my notebook and pen, and marched back outside.

Feodor had gathered the others on the street, and they were lost in a discussion of where, exactly, we should all go. I hovered on the edge of the group, and it was soon settled that a particular bakery a fifteen-minute walk away served the best bread and muffins, and as it was early in the day, that seemed to be the best choice.

I kept to the very back of the group, lagging so far behind that I had to jog to catch up. More often than I cared to admit, I searched out Feodor in the group, though he was almost always surrounded, eager Charges leaping at the chance to pick his brain and make an impression on the son of the Guild's next Elder. In a way, our adventure yesterday, despite the dark turn it had taken, felt like an honour now. How thrilled would these other young folk be to have such an opportunity?

He didn't once glance my way.

I grounded myself by staring up at the sky – or what we called the sky. There were no clouds, no sun, no stars at night. Just a blue-grey haze during the day, and a dark blur at night. Just nothingness, hanging above and around us, and the endless sense of moving.

At the bakery, we were seated at a long table with

benches running on either side. There weren't enough seats, and I pulled a chair from a nearby table and found myself a spot on the corner. No one seemed to notice, which was just fine with me.

I opened my notebook and took stock of each of the Charges in turn, as Fredek had asked. There were three girls and three boys, all dressed in the same rich green robes. Though they spoke amongst themselves, their eyes darted frequently to Feodor, checking if he had heard whatever deeply intelligent thing they had just said. He was *technically* a Charge, just like them, but with his father and his boundless magic, everyone in the city wanted to be his friend.

Semyon was the worst, speaking loudly and quoting the Magic Code in a way that ensured everyone could hear him.

As Official Fredek had requested, I began to take notes, beginning with Semyon.

Semyon. Speaks loudly. Frequently interrupts. Likes attention.

One of the girls, I noticed, was quiet and thoughtful, listening more than she spoke. I was sure to write it down. I made small sketches too – Fredek hadn't told me I shouldn't do that, but if anything it would only make the notes more interesting for him to read. I made notes about them all.

All except for Feodor, whose gaze I carefully avoided.

61

Not that he was searching mine out. He was a map enchanter. All the others present were map enchanters. I was barely a Clerk, here to take notes.

Velyo seems smarter than he lets on. He listens a lot, but he should probably talk more.

"Did you hear about that poor enchanter?" Velyo asked. The others shook their heads. "Vanished without a trace. A botched mapping job, they said. He was a Guild member too. Awful. Imagine it."

A few of the Charges shuddered.

"That's terrible," Feodor said sombrely. "I hope they find him."

The owner brought out two loaves of honey bread and a plate of oat muffins with water. The Charges all ravenously dug in, and I slipped a small muffin on to my plate when they'd finished grabbing and slicing. The chatter around the table softened some while people ate.

"So, who here has a favourite map enchanter from the old days?" said Feodor. "Perhaps someone you look up to, aspire to be like. Inessa, I heard you mention Brana just now?"

Inessa, the loudest of the three girls, with lustrous brown hair, flashed a radiant smile. "I was. Brana was the one true map enchanter. The first, besides Fedir. As such, she demands a certain respect. Few others have as many books written about them."

I risked a quick look at Feodor. He nodded slightly. Did the answer bore him, or was he refusing to show favouritism?

"That's what everyone says," Semyon said, as though the whole room had been awaiting his verdict. Inessa bristled, but maintained a smile. "If you were to ask the same question of anyone on the street, nine out of ten people would say Brana. But Brana's son, Eduard – he did more for map enchanting than anyone in history. He founded the Guild. He helped to define magic's limits. That takes a certain kind of person. A person who demands respect."

"Eduard would not have existed without Brana," Inessa countered softly. There was an edge to her voice. Maybe she wasn't boring, after all. Anyone who spoke to Semyon that way had to be all right in my book.

"That's a fact of nature. Nothing more," Semyon said. I found myself glaring at him and looked back down to my notepad, rage burning my ears.

"What do you think?" said Feodor, but no one replied. When I looked up, I found everyone looking at me.

"What do I think about what?"

"Who do you favour – as far as map enchanters go?" There was a hint of a smile in his eyes.

"Oh. I—" I caught Semyon's enraged expression. It was painfully clear he couldn't understand why Feodor had thought to address a Clerk. "Baba Yaga," I said, and smiled, satisfied. That ought to shock at least some in the room.

Baba Yaga was not someone to be respected. I knew that very well.

There were a few sudden intakes of breath, and Inessa whispered something to the other girl – what was her name? Madja? I hadn't yet caught it for my notes.

"Baba Yaga," Feodor said, and I knew from my brief interaction with him yesterday that he was amused.

"Yes. This is about map magic, no? Well, who deserves more respect than the woman who bound an entire city to a map and doomed it to never be found again? The power that must have taken is unimaginable." I had said it to be truculent, but the more I spoke, the more believable it sounded.

"That's … blasphemy," Semyon breathed. "Against the Guild. Against magic. Against Shard."

"Is it?" I looked at Feodor.

"Most of the dreygas were already banished to the Bleaks. She had no reason to do what she did to us. No reason to curse the city. How can you even say her name?" Semyon's face was redder than I had ever seen it before.

"It's unusual, Semyon," Feodor said slowly, "but Siya is not wrong. It was a question without right or wrong answers. Respecting magic and the things it can do means respecting *all* who have magic, even if you disagree with how they choose to use it. I believe we can all disagree with how Baba Yaga chose to use it."

"Then perhaps," said the girl who I was fairly certain

by this point was Madja, "she would like to explain her reasoning."

I swallowed and sat up straighter. "Well, it's just as Feodor said. We have yet to find another with as much map magic as Baba Yaga held. Could you, for example" – I turned to look directly at Semyon – "accomplish what she did? I would say it's unlikely. We cannot avoid the errors of the past without first understanding them."

Semyon did not break my gaze. "But I *do* think someone else could do what she did," he countered. "And it is presumptuous of you to think otherwise, seeing as you have no understanding of magic."

"It doesn't take magic to know that," I told him evenly. "Just a touch of common sense." Semyon bristled. Feodor hid a smile, which only egged me on. "Unless, of course, you think *you* hold that much power, Semyon? I know you hold yourself in high regard." *Shut up, Siya. Shut up.*

Semyon's chin edged higher. "I do hold myself in high regard," he breathed. "I am brimming with magic. It's everywhere. In every vein." He held up his hands above the table, turning them over. "In every breath I take. And where is it in you, Clerk? Where is it in you?"

I only stared at him.

"It's nowhere, Clerk. It's *nowhere* in you."

"Semyon." Feodor spoke sharply, but Semyon ignored him.

"You think that what Baba Yaga did was special? All

it takes is practice. Anyone can become like her. Anyone can become like the great ones who went before us. All you have to do is take the power you are born with, and hone it into something stronger. Watch." In a flash, he had snatched my notebook away and begun sketching something I couldn't quite see. Feodor stood quickly from his chair.

"Semyon!"

But Semyon didn't hear him, or didn't listen. He carried on sketching and speaking under his breath, and something in the room began to change. And then I realized. The door had disappeared.

Feodor stormed around the table and snatched the notebook away from Semyon. Semyon's lips continued to move, until Feodor clapped a hand over his mouth and shouted, loud enough to rattle the room, "*Semyon!*"

Then, at last, the room fell silent. The other Charges looked at each other, unsure of what to say. I gently took my notebook back from Feodor, as Semyon settled into his seat and smoothed back his hair.

"I was only trying to prove a point," he said quietly.

"I warned you to stop. Now look what you've done." He swept a hand to the door of the bakery, which had completely vanished.

The owner had emerged from the back kitchen and was staring in shock at the place where his door had been. "What have you done? There's no door! I must have a door!"

He felt around the wall where it should be, as though perhaps he could find it hidden amongst the boards of the wall.

"Fear not," Feodor told him. "I will fix it. It was only a mistake. I can assure you that it will not happen again."

We all watched silently as Feodor made the door reappear. The owner, too relieved to complain any further, thanked him profusely, and propped the door open to let in the day's air.

"We should be off," Feodor said, turning back to the Charges. "I think we've done enough for one day." His eyes landed again on Semyon. The other Charges went out, and I hung back, gathering my things as slowly as I could.

"I would…" Semyon cleared his throat. "I would be grateful if you didn't bring this up with the Magisters. Or anyone. It was a mistake, and one I won't make again."

If only I could have seen how red his face must have gone, to be begging so.

"You were reckless," Feodor told him. "Dangerous."

"Your good opinion will go a long way with the Guild."

"I'm afraid you haven't done much to earn that," Feodor told him, but I could hear the forgiveness in his voice.

"I will keep trying."

"Off with you." Feodor nodded towards the door. For a moment, it was just the two of us, and he gave me a long, tired look. I thought he might say something, make a funny comment about how the outing had gone, or a reference to the events of yesterday, which I was growing more and more certain had only been a dream.

But instead, Feodor drew in a long breath, let it out, and left the building.

5

*The city gardens, at the end of the day. Meet me by
the Starlight Trees, if you please.*

I read the message for the hundredth time, then put it
back in my pocket. Then pulled it out again for the hundredth
and first. To see if it still said what I thought it had said.

The message had arrived perhaps an hour after my
return from the outing with the Charges. It must be from
Feodor, but I didn't know why he wanted to see me again.
He'd hardly looked my way during the Charge outing.

Maybe the purpose of the meeting was to chastise me
for what I'd said about Baba Yaga. We were not meant to
appreciate Baba Yaga in any way, but, in the moment, I had
felt the desire to be outrageous. Shocking. To say something
to upset Semyon.

Like a child would.

It is important, Siya, that we always show the Charges the proper way to be. What it truly means to revere magic. To laud the great ones who came before us, and fear the ones who tried to ruin us.

I had scolded myself through an imaginary Feodor's voice over and over again, trying to guess just the way he might do so given my brief interactions with him.

In the end, I shoved the note deep into my pocket and tried to put it from my mind. The scolding would come soon enough. No use wasting a day thinking of nothing else.

Though I couldn't say exactly why, I stayed a little longer at the Guild, filing and refiling old papers until the outside light trailing into the main foyer began to fall, signalling that the sun was setting somewhere beyond the bounds of our captive city. Perhaps I had lingered a bit in the hope of seeing my father again. He had spoken to me only once since I'd come upon them with Feodor, telling me I had been rude to enter without knocking, and to do better next time.

Nothing of what had actually been going on.

As the world grew ever darker, I sighed. I could no longer put it off; it was time to meet Feodor.

What if I just didn't go at all?

But that was ridiculous. I wasn't scared of Feodor. Was I?

I stopped on the steps outside to breathe in the evening, to soak in the peace that came with a dying day. The wash of grey that served as the sky of our city had turned dark, and if I stared for long enough, I could imagine stars. There were no beautiful sunsets. No blue skies that melted into orange, then grey. Only light to dark. Colourless and empty.

The Guild had never quite been able to explain how it was that the sky lightened and darkened, even though we could see no sun or moon. The thinking was that we were still somewhere within the limits of Sarsova, wandering endlessly like a snowstorm, but could still be bound by the darkness brought by their setting sun. When Sarsova grew dark, Shard grew dark. Sunsets, however, held far less magic if there was no sun to behold.

If you were to try to walk through the city gates, you would smack into an invisible wall. I'd been to see it once, and if you didn't know about the invisible wall, it would look like you were about to step off into midnight and fall for ever.

I collected myself, and hurried down the steps to the street that headed towards the gardens.

The cobblestones were bustling with folk heading home for the day, though they emptied more and more the further I walked, as people seeped into their homes. The walk led me down one of my favourite streets in the city: a row of timber-framed houses that all looked like cookie-cutter copies of one another, but with small differences if you looked hard enough. A dried flower wreath on one door. A candle in the window of another. A bird's nest propped

71

up against that one's chimney. A door that stood slightly crooked.

It was a happy street, with happy houses, and I found it nearly impossible to be in a foul mood while walking down it.

The gardens sat near the heart of the city, in the distant shadow of the Snowfall Palace. I came to these parts rarely. There was something about the wilted Starlight Trees – trees that had once bloomed bright and brilliant at night, by the dim light cast by a hundred million stars in Sarsova – which always brought me a wave of bitter sadness.

The trees were dotted haphazardly about, making a small forest in the middle of the city. Beneath them grew grass and small blue flowers that crept along the ground. It held its own sort of magic, this place. And maybe that's why it was so sad: it was the most magical place in the city, and yet it could never again reach its full potential while we were still adrift.

Feodor sat waiting for me on a wooden bench beneath one of the trees. One foot rested atop his other leg, and his arm was stretched out over the back of the bench. In the failing light, his dark red coat seemed almost black. I approached slowly.

"It's quite a night."

I stopped walking. Cleared my throat. "It would be better if there were stars." I looked up the vast, dark blue expanse beyond us.

"It is still beautiful, just as it is," Feodor said, craning his neck to look up too. "Sometimes I think if we had stars and a sun, we would have less to dream about. I like trying to imagine it."

I stepped closer to his bench. "It's polite to ask me to sit."

"Ah. Your favourite word. Sit, then, Siya. You don't strike me as the sort of person who waits for an invitation."

"I didn't want to be presumptuous."

"Please, be presumptuous, with my blessing."

Something in the way he said it tickled my spine.

I sat down, aware of the small space between us. "Why did you ask me come here?" I asked. "To have a stern word with me, out of earshot of any Charges?"

"Why would I have a stern word with you?"

"I—" I started talking, then stopped, confused. "Because of what I said about Baba Yaga."

He looked surprised, as if he had forgotten about what I had said. "It's not my place to tell you what you should and should not say, Siya. If anything, I agreed with you."

I looked away from him, head swimming. He agreed with me.

Sitting up straighter, I asked, "If you didn't plan to scold me, then why ask me here? Why here and not the Guild?"

Feodor leaned forward, resting his elbows on his knees. His eyes roamed around the gardens. "To be away from prying eyes and ears."

I leaned in closer. "Whose eyes and ears?"

"The Guild's."

I blinked at him. Feodor Sevastyen, a boy full of map magic, revered by everyone, likely to one day be an Elder, holding a covert meeting out of earshot of the Guild. These were dangerous waters leading to uncharted territories. And, unsettling as they were, an inviting and delicious wind filled my sails.

I smiled, just a little. "This sounds like trouble. I like trouble."

He sat back again. The ease and composure he had shown in the Sanctum was gone, and I saw the strain on his face. "Something isn't right," he said, so quietly I barely heard it above the song of the evening birds. "Something has not been right for a while, if I'm honest."

A cool breeze toyed with my hair, but I was too rapt to fix it.

"I have spent the past day thinking of every possible reason why the Magisters would hide a piece of the map. The map everyone in Shard has worked to find. *Why* is it a secret? And what were the Magisters doing when we found them? I can't get it out of my mind. I can't move past it. And my father has been ... odd, for some time."

I watched his face. "Perhaps they worry the map might be stolen."

"They are the Guild," he said. "They could bury it so deeply under map magic it would be like it never existed at all. They can hide anything, anywhere. They do not fear thievery."

"Why do people ever keep secrets?" I mused aloud, staring into the now-dark Starlight Trees. "Because they have something to gain by keeping them, or something to lose by giving them up."

"So, what we have to find out," Feodor said, leaning closer and dropping his voice to a whisper again, "is what the Guild has to gain by keeping this secret."

"We," I said, suddenly aware of how close he sat. "How will *we* find that out?"

For a moment, Feodor said nothing, only looked at me, thinking.

Then he blinked, sat back, and said, "Well, I suppose we wait and see what the Guild does once they find out their piece is missing. What they say. And … the rest of the map must be somewhere in the city. The pieces can't come and go if we can't. If we could piece it back together…" He drew in a breath. "I want to see what happens when we send Shard back to Sarsova."

"So, what's your plan? We scour every inch of the city? Turn over every cobblestone, search through every house? Anyone could have it, waiting until the right time to say so. Waiting to be a hero, or to sell it. The Guild will find it before we do, if they're searching for it." The city around us seemed to expand as I spoke, a never-ending series of streets and alleys and tunnels and houses that would take lifetimes to search.

"No," Feodor said thoughtfully, "we would never have the time to search the city. We should start back in the Guild. The Magisters must have some clue or lead they've been following. And a reason to keep it a secret."

"What if we get caught?" The Guild would not take kindly to us poking around where we didn't belong, especially after our run-in with the Magisters.

Feodor's mouth twisted in a vicious smile. "We can't get caught."

The smile vanished in an instant, and his eyes moved past me to focus on something else. I turned, following his gaze to see what had unsettled him — and saw the distant form of a woman, drenched in a dark cloak, standing between two trees.

Watching us.

Despite her distance, I could feel her gaze flickering on us like embers from a fire. I remembered my walk back from the house call, and the feeling of being watched then.

"Were you expecting someone else?" I asked, still watching her.

Beside me, Feodor shook his head. "No. I've never seen her before."

With sure, purposeful steps, the woman began to move towards us, melting in and out of the darkness around the trees until she reached the road where our bench sat. She cast a glance up and down it before stepping on to the stones, then approached much slower, leaving maybe ten feet between us.

When she had stopped walking, she pulled her hood back, just enough so we could barely see her face in the darkness.

I didn't know her, but she was beautiful – light hair braided back away from her face, eyes as piercing as a knife.

Feodor stood, so I followed. Almost imperceptibly, the woman nodded once to us.

"Good evening," she said. Her voice was rich and heavy, and lovely.

"Evening," Feodor said. His fists were clenched, his jaw set tightly.

"Is this important?" I asked, hiding my uncertainty beneath impudence. "We were speaking."

"I will keep this short," the woman replied. She glanced around. There was no one close by, only a few stragglers enjoying the last remnants of the evening in the garden far away. "My name is Viveka, and I know you were in the Sanctum."

All of the brashness I'd just felt deserted me.

"I don't know what you mean," Feodor whispered, as if our fathers were listening.

"Oh, save us all some time," Viveka said, dismissively waving a hand. "I saw you go in, and I saw you leave. That's that."

I shifted from one foot to the other. "You aren't a member of the Guild," I said.

"No," she said, looking over her shoulder quickly, as though a noise had startled her. "I am not a member of the Guild. Not any more, at least. I used to work in the Sanctum. But things ended very badly, and now they have something of mine. I want to get it back."

A bird called close by, sharply, causing us all to start.

"What?" Feodor asked.

Viveka dropped her voice even lower. "I need your help releasing a prisoner from the Guild."

I could have recited the opening page of the *Annals of the Guild of Map Magic* in the silence that followed.

"I didn't know they had prisoners," Feodor said slowly. "The occasional infraction of the City Code might warrant someone a night locked up, but somehow I don't think that's what you mean."

"No. That is not what I mean. They have someone down there and I want to get him back."

"Oh," I said. "This sounds like a lover."

"Yes," she replied, her tone softening. "His name is Farod. I am forbidden from entering the Guild. I have been watching it – that's how I saw you both. But I can't go inside. The Guild wouldn't let me leave."

I frowned. "That doesn't sound like the Guild."

She looked sadly into my eyes. "Then you don't know them very well."

I fell silent.

"There is no one else I can ask for help and to trust with my secret. You two, sneaking around together, breaking the rules – you seemed like the best choice. All I had, really."

"The secret is that the Guild is keeping your lover as a prisoner?" I said, trying to keep up.

"No," Feodor said, looking intently at Viveka. "I think she means another secret."

Viveka eyed him for a moment. "Yes," she said. "Another secret."

Birds called. Distant laughter floated to us on the evening air. We waited for Viveka to continue.

"Farod," she said, so quietly I almost didn't hear her, "is a dreyga."

Feodor took a step back, nearly stumbling over the bench. I, on the other hand, couldn't move. Her words echoed in my head. *Dreyga. Farod is a dreyga.*

The city spoke so rarely of dreygas now. Cut off as we were, their danger had slipped away into memory, into bedtime stories and whispers. Stories I had read in the Atheneum, ones my father had told to my brother and sister and I when we'd grown old enough to hear them, came rushing back. Human-like monsters who feasted on magic and left their victims for dead. Creatures that drained magic from the living and left nothing but husks behind. They could sense it. Smell it. Consume it. And they desired nothing more.

"There are no dreygas in the city any more. They were killed when Baba Yaga banished us," Feodor said.

"There are," Viveka said, as confidently as if she were saying water was wet. "But it's the Guild's little secret. A carefully guarded secret. Like I said, I was once a member of the Guild. I worked in the Sanctum, checking on the dreyga and guarding his cell. I got to know him, and…"

She fell in love with him, I thought. With a monster.

I had never in my life heard anyone describe a dreyga as anything close to human. *They eat people's magic,* I wanted to say, but of course she would know that.

"I tried very hard to set him free. Had it all planned out, carefully, over months. We were so close. But the Guild caught us. I managed to escape, barely, but if they ever catch me again, knowing that I'm carrying their secret around the city… I don't know what will happen."

"Why," I asked, "would the Guild keep a dreyga?"

"Their reasons are beyond me and my knowledge," she said. "I just want to get Farod back. He was once my everything, and without him, I am nothing."

There was a tremor in her voice, a richness born only from love. Yet who could love a dreyga?

"Was there more than one?" I asked quietly. "More than your dreyga?"

"I don't know," she replied. "They broke up secrets between people, so no one knew too much. I knew about Farod, and I loved him."

"We can't help you," Feodor told her plainly, "because there is no reason we would ever *release a dreyga* from Guild captivity. Especially not one that we are not even meant to know about."

I gave her a half-hearted *what can you do?* shrug. Because of course Feodor was right. Maybe I had my suspicions of the Guild and their secrets, but taking out my frustrations by releasing a magic-devouring beast felt extreme. "I think you'll have to find someone else to commit crimes for you."

"I can think of a reason for you to help me," she said. "More than one reason. Let's start with how I can tell the Guild about your foray into the Sanctum, with enough detail that they'll have to believe me. I can find someone who will believe me and who has the Magisters' ear. Let me think... What is his name ... Semyon? He would go to the Magisters at once."

I let out a breath through my teeth.

"Besides, you haven't heard what I could give you in return."

"Don't keep us in suspense," I said, wondering what she could offer that would make freeing a magic-sucking beast worth it.

She said, "I think I might know where one of the missing pieces of the map can be found. With it, you can save the city. Be the heroes you so clearly want to be."

An ugly choking sound came from my throat. Without thinking, I reached out for Feodor's wrist. Our eyes met. Neither of us spoke, but a conversation tumbled out in the silence. This was it. Everything I had been dreaming of without allowing myself to think it could one day be real.

The chance to *do* something. All those days locked away in the dusty Guild office, dreaming of something bigger, something better.

This was it. This was the something better.

We had to piece the map back together. Save the city.

There was the piece hanging in the Guild. There was the piece Feodor and I had stolen. All we needed was the last piece.

"We have to," I whispered, staring so intently into Feodor's eyes I felt almost certain I could read his thoughts. "We *have to*."

"But what she asks in return, Siya… It's too great a price."

"I can assure you that Farod will cause no harm to anyone in the city," Viveka said. "I will make sure of that."

I gestured to her in a way that said, *See? There is little to lose, and so much to gain.*

Feodor bit his lip, rocking from one foot, to the other. "But if that isn't true, and he kills someone, Siya, that blood will be on our hands. Their life, lost, because of us. Could you live with that?"

The weight of his words was like a heavy stone placed on my chest – but the lightness of hope somehow felt stronger.

"But what you could gain, Feodor, think of it!" I said. "Saving Shard. Returning us to Sarsova, to a land with forests and animals and stars. I dream of a sky, Feodor, at night, every night. I dream of stars and a moon and a sun to wake up to. I want the world the gods promised us long ago. I want it back. We can get it back."

He removed his arm from my grasp. "Why should we trust you?" Feodor asked Viveka. "You say you know where the rest of the map hides. Then why haven't you found it before? Why would you tell us?"

"You hear things, over time," said Viveka. "Things people say when they don't know you're there. I realized how useful it could be. Some people pay for things with money or magic, but I have neither. So, I deal in secrets. If anyone in the city wants to know something about the Guild, I can get it. I have a solid rumour tucked away up here" – she tapped her temple – "about where a piece of the map is kept. I've been holding on to it for the right time. So I can exchange it for something I want. And I think I've found it."

Farod's freedom.

"And we get no proof, I presume," Feodor said, lacing his fingers behind his head. "Just your word to go on, is it?"

Viveka gave a dark smile. "I don't need to offer proof. I can ruin you if you refuse."

"Telling the Guild we were in the Sanctum is hardly ruining us," Feodor said, but there was an edge of worry to his voice.

"Perhaps not, but telling them you *stole* something from the Sanctum would."

Feodor inhaled sharply. I watched as they gazed at each

other intently. One free dreyga, in exchange for our freedom and the city's safety. Surely, Feodor would agree.

"So," Viveka said. "Will you free Farod?"

Feodor looked at me. I tried to keep my face blank and filled my heart with hope instead. Hope that I might one day see the stars flung about the sky beyond. Feel snow tumbling from branches of trees that seemed to touch the sky. Hope that one day, I could run through the city gates and run and run and run without stopping through the fields and glens and forests that had been a part of Sarsova since time immemorial.

Hope was all I had to give.

"Yes," Feodor finally said, the word a cool wave amidst crushing heat. "Yes. We will try and free the dreyga."

Without thinking, I lunged forward and wrapped my arms around him, nestling my face, for the briefest of moments, into the crook of his neck.

Then I remembered myself and darted backwards, my face and ears hot. Feodor stared at me, mouth open, and I wanted nothing more than for the ground to open up and swallow me whole.

"I'm not embarrassed," I said quickly, to cover my embarrassment.

"I didn't think you were."

"Right," Viveka said. "Meet me at the old church the day after he's released. Noontime. I will tell you where to find it."

"Wait. Wait." Feodor held up his hands as if to say *not so fast*. "Why don't you tell us now?"

"If I tell you now, then I'll have no reason to trust you. So, one of us must trust the other." She stepped in a bit closer. "But if the rumour is correct, then I do know where it is. It's in the hands of someone, somewhere in this city. In fact, you aren't far from it right now."

Instinctively, I turned to look all around us, as though I might find it flapping in the breeze up in one of the trees.

Viveka smiled and stepped back. "Best of luck to you – and be careful."

Her words hung haunting and heavy in the air as she disappeared into the Starlight Trees, and though I'd been relieved when Feodor had agreed to the bargain, a creeping, haunting dread began to settle into my heart as I watched her go.

6

From the shadows of a great pillar in the foyer, I watched a group of Magisters, my father included, make their way up the stairs and disappear. Their black robes whispered lightly on the floor, and, around the neck of a man whose name I couldn't place, I saw the edge of a necklace slip out for the briefest of moments before he tucked it back in. Just like the one I had seen my father wearing.

Tell me your secrets. I imagined storming across the foyer and demanding answers from them.

I had told Official Fredek that Feodor wanted to speak about the Charge outing, and he had waved me away distractedly, too busy to pay me much attention.

As I made my way down the ornate, curved steps towards the Atheneum below the Guild, the steps that had always brought me a tingle of joy and excitement, I felt nothing. Now that I knew what things lurked beneath it, I felt certain in my bones that it would never have the same charm again. Dark secrets have a way of tainting things like that.

Inside the great book-shaped doors, Yarik stood behind his desk, making notes and humming to himself.

"No nap today, Yarik?" I asked.

He harrumphed, and adjusted his glasses. "I don't know what you mean." There was a hint of a smile in his eyes.

"If you say so. Don't mind me, I'm just collecting something for Official Fredek."

He glanced at me, but then returned to his humming. Yarik was used to me making my way about, darting in and out of the Atheneum, sometimes lurking for much longer than I should. Even so, I let out a sigh of relief as I hurried past his desk.

I slowed as I neared the bookshelves that weren't bookshelves – the door to the Sanctum. I had been here only days before, but since then everything felt altered. The way I thought things were, the world I thought I was a part of, it had all slipped away and left something unfamiliar in its place.

A bit dramatic, don't you think? I could hear Feodor's voice in my head. Still, a little drama couldn't hurt, after years of monotony. Might as well soak up all the excitement I could before things returned to normal.

If they returned to normal.

Today, there were a few other occupants in the Atheneum. A small group of Charges pored over a large book, speaking softly. Beside a ladder, two Clerks stood gossiping, books propped in their arms, frequently glancing towards the doors as though they really must be getting back to work. Everyone, though, was focused on something other than me.

I took a deep breath, positioned myself just out of everyone's line of sight, turned the key in the lock, and slipped quietly through the bookshelves.

My hands trembled as I reached for the rail along the winding, coiled stairway. *If Viveka saw me last time, who might have seen me this time?*

"Hello, Siya."

Feodor caught up with me on the stairs, silently.

"You were brave to come," he said.

"No braver than you," I said, turning away to carry on down the stairs.

"I nearly didn't," he admitted. "This isn't exactly … a light undertaking."

I wasn't sure if his words made me feel better or worse.

"The Magisters are busy today," he said as we walked. "Busier than usual. I don't know why. I've barely caught a glimpse of my father all day, but we can't trust that it will last."

"I saw them leaving the Atheneum," I told him.

"They might come back," he said. "And they will likely know we're here before we even know they are coming."

I shivered. Gods above and below, how convenient magic could be.

The stairway finally ended, and again the dingy grey stone hall opened up before us. This time, Feodor wasted no time in transforming it into the Sanctum that lay hidden behind magic; arched doorways and metal sconces appearing suddenly where seconds ago, there had been nothing.

I tried to hide how impressed I was. If there was one thing that Feodor did *not* need, it was another person telling him how talented he was.

If only we could use his magic to break directly into the cell where Farod was being kept, but the Guild had long ago ensured that no one could break in with magic. You could leave, but you couldn't enter. The only way in to where we needed to go was through the magical version of the Sanctum, which now stood before us.

I pulled a torch free from where it hung on the wall, a bit aggressively, and forced a loud sigh. "I think I left my nerves upstairs," I told him.

He smiled, but only half-heartedly.

We had stopped, and now faced the doorway that led towards that awful sound we had heard the other day. The sound I had not been able to push from my mind. The sound that had haunted my dreams.

"I don't know what awaits us, exactly," Feodor said. To my surprise, he reached out and squeezed my hand and

I did nothing to pull it away. "I have never met a dreyga before, other than in the pages of books. But we will do this together. I can always use magic to get us out, as long as I have enough time. So stay close. You understand?"

"Yes, sir," I said smartly. Feodor gave me a long, serious look and I sighed. "Yes, I understand."

Then, together, we stepped through the doorway and into the dark hallway that waited beyond.

The ground became rougher with every step. The arched doorways ceased, and in their place were uneven walls, circles cut out that led into cells so dark it was like midnight with your eyes closed. The torch I had lit on one of the sconces by the stairway was the only light, and what was before us lay shrouded in a thick, inky darkness. Shapes seemed to form in the shadows, faces and forms and teeth lurking just beyond sight. Sweat dripped from my forehead into my eyes, even though the air was cold and damp. Here and there, stones lay in piles where a wall had crumbled or part of the ceiling had fallen in.

This place was *old*. The people who had built it likely now lived only in books that were hard to open without the pages crumbling. The very air felt arcane. Like I was trespassing on forbidden ground. Ground that had managed to keep its secrets for centuries.

"I've heard whispers," Feodor said. "Rumours of a part of the Guild so ancient it predates the city. Predates everything we know. Hallowed halls built centuries ago, that most people can never find."

"I think we've found it," I said, brushing a cobweb from my sleeve. We passed empty cell after empty cell.

"I suppose it is the right place to keep a dreyga, if one were to keep a dreyga," he said. "No one comes here. No one knows it's here."

"What do you suppose it will look like?" I asked.

"Perhaps best not to speculate. We will know soon enough."

Without warning, my feet drew to a stop. I felt it, up ahead. A presence, heavy like honey, dark as black melted wax. It consumed everything, all the air around me, the light in my hand, the thoughts in my mind. It was everywhere, in everything, and although I could see nothing myself, I knew it could see me.

"I think we've found him," Feodor whispered.

Every bit of me wanted to turn back. Turn back and *run*. But we had come so far, and the chance might not come around again. The final piece of the map was nearly within our grasp, I was sure of it, and to leave would be to give up on everything we had hoped for. Everything the city had hoped for. Everything I hoped for.

This was the right thing to do. I was sure of it. Shard needed saving, after so long wandering. So long without a home. And it's not doing the right thing if you aren't a little bit scared.

So I stood up straighter, and I moved forward.

I swung the torch forward to illuminate the cell, and the light fell on *something* that forced a cry from my chest. Pale skin clung to a gaunt frame, one that sat on the floor, staring at us with dim, amber eyes. It looked human, for the most part, but only barely. Skeletal and tall and with fingernails that had grown far too long. But all the familiar features were there. Eyes and nose and mouth and hair. It could be hard, at first, to distinguish him from anyone else after merely a glance.

I had never met a dreyga before, but I knew it was hungry just from a first glance. Starving.

"Farod," I said softly, and his head turned in my direction, those eyes piercing my skin. His movements were sudden and stark, but somehow all too human.

Feodor moved to stand close by my elbow, his breathing loud in the silence.

"Farod," I said again, my voice firmer this time. "That's your name, isn't it?"

He rose slowly, without looking away. Almost imperceptibly, his eyes moved from me to Feodor, and his hunger started to visibly burn there, the amber flaring to life like candles. All the things I had ever heard about dreygas came back – their desire for magic, their need for it, the way they could drink it from a body and leave someone for dead.

I moved to stand between them.

"Nobody knows my name," Farod said, his voice thick and guttural, as if rain-soaked rocks could speak.

"Viveka knows it."

In an instant, Farod had rushed across the cell and held fast to the bars, pressing his face against them. "Viveka," he hissed. "What do you know of Viveka?"

"We spoke with her," I answered. Feodor had taken the torch, and I clasped my hands together to stop them shaking. Feodor looked back up the hall to ensure that we were still alone. "She asked us to free you."

Farod's lips peeled back to reveal a smile, sharp, silvery teeth glinting in the torchlight. "Free me," he echoed, his eyes taking on a dreamy look. "I hardly remember freedom."

"If we free you, Farod, you must agree to our conditions. Viveka has promised us you will kill no one. *No one.* You will not take even one magical life."

"Then how will I survive?"

"That isn't my concern. If you kill anyone, the Guild will not only keep you as their prisoner next time," I told him, as though I had any conception of what the Guild might do with their captive dreyga. "They will kill you."

A heartbeat of silence slipped by. Feodor looked nervously up the hall again.

"I will not kill," Farod whispered, and his voice rose bumps along my skin. He dipped his head to me in a nod that felt like some sort of promise. I returned it awkwardly, still shaking.

I looked to Feodor. Was it time? Were we to release a *dreyga* into the city? Distantly, a soft noise reached us, and Feodor jumped, the light from the torch dancing wildly.

"We have to go," he said quickly, pulling a piece of parchment from his pocket. With swift fingers, he sketched the hall and the cell on to the page, Farod watching intently. Before the sketch was even finished, the incantation began to tumble out of Feodor, and I stepped back to give him space, though I wasn't sure why. Second by second, the door of the cell began to fade, until, in an instant, it was gone. The bars that Farod had clung to vanished, and he tumbled to the floor, swiftly standing again.

He carried himself with an odd grace – the grace of something almost human but not entirely. A tattered old brown leather coat hung down to his knees, and a pair of worn boots with missing laces and plentiful holes covered what I assumed were mostly normal feet. His fingernails were too long, reminding me a bit of talons, and I kept my eyes from them before my imagination ran too wild. He stood taller than me by half a metre.

He placed one foot outside the perimeter of the cell and stared at it. A moment later, he moved the other, until the whole of his form stood with us in the hallway. That heavy presence drew closer.

His ragged brown coat looked too small, like it had been stripped from the body of someone he had killed and he'd worn it ever since. The thought turned my stomach.

Farod's eyes roved around, overwhelmed, until they settled on Feodor and stayed there. I kept my body between them.

"You can't do it," Feodor said. *You can't kill me*, was what he meant. "You will never leave the Guild alive."

I stepped forward, closer to the dreyga, who watched me move like a bird watched things move on the ground. "Leave. Now," I said. "I don't know where this hallway goes, but I'm certain you can find a crack to slip through. Stay out of sight. Find Viveka. And don't kill anyone."

Farod sucked in a heavy breath, staring at me.

"I mean it," I added, this time in a whisper.

For a moment, I thought he might say something, his mouth open as if he were about to speak. The sharp points of his teeth were just barely visible. But instead, he turned away from us, and fled down the hall in a run so fast he had vanished in the space of a heartbeat.

7

I stared after Farod. His departure had sucked the air from the hallway, and his absence left me feeling dizzy, like I was in the grey space between waking and dreaming.

It wasn't until Feodor grabbed hold of my hand that I came to myself.

"Come on," he said roughly. "Can you hear that?"

The noises from behind us were getting louder – the sound of footsteps. Someone else was in the tunnel with us. We couldn't go back, so we had to go on, in the direction Farod had gone. We didn't know where it led, or what we might find, but going back would only see us caught.

So we hurried on, in silence.

There was nothing to say. We had released a dreyga into the City of Shard. Yes, we had done it in the hope of saving the city from this endless wandering, but still, we had unleashed a terrible thing.

As long as Viveka held true to her word, it would be worth it. I knew it would.

A little voice that sometimes fought its way through to the forefront of my mind worried, *What if you did do all of this selfishly? You've been looked over all these years. Ignored. Pushed aside, because you have no magic.* Maybe putting the magical people of the city in danger made me feel a tiny bit powerful.

I shut down that voice. We would piece the map back together, and the city would finally return, glistening and vibrant, back to Sarsova where it belonged. One dreyga, in the whole of the city, was a small price to pay for such a thing. Once Shard was restored to Sarsova, we could find Farod again and banish him to the Bleaks, with the rest of the dreygas, and no one would be harmed. So long as no one wandered into the mountains, the dreygas could never harm them. And no one accidentally wandered into the Bleaks, knowing what lived there.

I couldn't help but wonder, though, if they really had been sent to the Bleaks, now that I knew Farod was still here. Were there more?

The ancient hallway unceremoniously came to an end at a pile of rocks. We both stopped and stood in silence for a long while. Each rock was larger than either of us and there were far too many to move. Overhead, very distantly, a sliver of light peeked through, but the rocks were too smooth to climb, and a fall would mean certain death.

"I suppose that's how Farod got out," Feodor said, eyeing the distant crack. I shivered, imagining his slender form climbing the rocks like a spider. "I think I can get us out, but I don't know where we'll find ourselves on the other side."

He withdrew more parchment from his coat and began to sketch the rocks, crouching to use his knee as a table.

"Feodor?" I said. "Do you think we did the right thing?"

A moment of silence slipped by. "Who's to say what's right and wrong?" He didn't look at me as he spoke. "Was the Guild right to keep a dreyga captive? Were we right to free it? What does right mean?"

"We might have put people in danger."

He sighed. "Yes. We might have. But we also might save the city."

Feodor smiled and stood up, finished with his drawing. "Either way, we've done it now. Come on. We need to get out and then lie low. Come up with some story about where we've been all day."

He began the incantation, and spoke swiftly. I stared at the rocks, waiting, still imagining Farod ascending them with the speed and grace of something inhuman.

One by one, a handful of the higher rocks began to vanish, leaving openings where grey daylight poured through.

We scaled the lower rocks, working together to pull each other up when needed. At last we found an opening that was wide enough to crawl through, and made it out into the open air.

The other side, it turned out, brought us into a remote edge of the city, next to a stagnant canal that was no longer used. A few run-down buildings stood nearby, but there wasn't a soul in sight, save for a stray dog that ran away at the first sign of our approach. The pile of rocks looked to passing eyes like the remnants of an ancient building, far beyond repair.

We sat for a while on the edge of the canal, watching flies land and take off again, reliving the past hour or so over and over again. I thought of what we had done, of Farod's voice, his eyes, the speed with which he had moved. Of how he had felt so very old. A sob bubbled up in my throat and Feodor put his arm around me, and we sat for a few minutes, scared but together.

"It's funny," I said through a few errant tears. "Adventure is so much more frightening when it isn't in a book."

We parted ways back in the city and I walked home alone. I found myself looking for signs of Farod, glancing down every side street, peering through dark doorways, certain I would see his tall form lurking somewhere. But life in the city was carrying on as usual – people bustling around, business being conducted, children playing. Nothing seemed out of place. No one seemed to have noticed that a dreyga now slipped amongst them.

I couldn't see the city the same way any more. It was as though the secrets I carried with me had given me a new kind of vision, one where I saw darkness everywhere. Shard wasn't Shard any more, at least not completely. Something – maybe everything – had forever changed.

And there was also the quiet little fear that someone in the Guild had seen us. That the next time I walked through the doors, someone would point at me and everything would fall apart. We had been careful, but how far ahead of us could the Guild be?

I stopped in one of the streets and leaned my back against the wall. We had agreed that returning to the Guild seemed like the safest thing to do. Make sure people saw us. Show that, as far as we knew, today was just a normal day.

Going back to the Guild to finish off the day's work, as unpleasant as it seemed given what I had just done, felt like a good distraction. I would need something to occupy my mind for the remainder of the day. Feodor might not be missed, seeing as he came and went so often. But my absence might be noted, especially by someone like Official Fredek if he went in search of me for some insignificant task.

With a heavy sigh, I pushed off the wall and slipped back through the city to the Guild.

In the foyer, everything was normal. My tiny office was just as I had left it. Nothing had changed.

That wouldn't last. *Someone* had been in the Sanctum when Feodor and I had left. We'd heard them. If they hadn't already communicated the news of the missing prisoner, they would do it soon.

There was nothing I could do now except keep my head down. So I filed papers, I transferred notes to a ledger, and I hummed all the while, the picture of ease, to hide the inner turmoil.

I remembered Feodor's words to me in the Sanctum the first time. An invitation to get into trouble together.

Come on. This way, we can get into trouble together.

It had seemed delicious and exciting then, before I learned just how much trouble we could find ourselves in. Did I regret it? I wasn't sure yet.

A ripple of gentle commotion began in the foyer outside. I swallowed. *It's starting.* I could hear the sound of running feet, see people rushing past my door.

"No, not here. Upstairs."

The voice of a familiar Magister filtered in as he and others hurried past my door.

"I told you, keep your voice down..."

Did they know it was me who had freed the prisoner?

I couldn't wait any longer. I chanced a brief glance up in time to see two Officials jogging by, their eyes wide.

My hand shook.

Don't be so dramatic. No one will suspect the girl with no magic, Siya. Why would anyone think you had anything to do with it?

But all I could think was: if the Guild was so bold as to keep a dreyga captive, what would they do to the person who let it go free?

"Siya."

I yelped and jumped, finding Official Fredek in the doorway.

"Forgive me," I said quickly, standing. "I was lost in thought."

"You may go home for the day. Something has come up and all non-essential people are to leave for the evening."

"Are you sure? Can I help with … whatever it is?"

"No, I'm afraid not." A short, nervous laugh. "I must go. I'll see you tomorrow, unless you hear otherwise." He left quickly.

I stood still for a long moment. Then I put away my papers, took my cloak from the wall, and closed the office door behind me. I peered around the corner into the foyer as I tied on my cloak, taking stock of exactly what the mood was.

And the mood, it seemed, was stifled chaos.

Officials and Magisters made hurriedly for the stairs leading down to the Atheneum and the Sanctum, while others ushered Clerks and Charges out of the great front doors. I heard snatches of "Nothing to worry about. All

102

under control" and "We'll see you tomorrow. Enjoy a surprise afternoon off!"

They didn't suspect me. Why would they? I was a nobody.

I smiled a little, satisfied, as I finished tying on my cloak and made my way across the foyer. There was no question now. The Guild knew about the missing dreyga.

My missing dreyga. The one I had set free.

Out on the streets, my smile faded. I walked slowly or far too quickly, peeking around the corners of alleyways before passing them, searching windows for any sign of Farod's face. It was silly, though: dreygas fed on magic, and I had no magic. But I couldn't forget that troubling, heavy presence.

Feodor wasn't a Magister, or even an Official, but with his talent and prominent father, would he become privy to the discussions about the missing dreyga? Would he be suspected, even questioned, or would the son of the next Elder be above suspicion? We had no Elder currently, the most recent one having died. As soon as the rest of the Guild had finished their questioning and induction period, Ermolai would take his place as the head of the Guild. Surely, being his son meant Feodor would be protected against almost anything.

I had dragged him into this. He had agreed to it, sure, but that didn't make me feel any better about it.

By the time I reached home, my body ached all over.

The stairs into the Sanctum, climbing the rocks to get out, and the endless shaking of fear had taken its toll.

"You're home early," my mother noted, tucking a few loose strands back into her braids. Her face was red from standing close to a warm oven.

"Yes. Official Fredek sent me home. A meeting or something. They were all quite busy."

"Is everything all right?" An edge of worry tinged her voice, but I bit back the truth.

"I think so. I'm sure Father will know more, later. If you don't mind, I'm going to go rest." I wanted to tell her everything, and the weight of the words pushing against my tongue propelled me up the stairs to my room.

I climbed into my bed, and closed my eyes until a restless sleep found me.

Father came home late, and very disturbed. It was late enough that I had slept my way through a series of strange, toothy dreams. I heard him greet Mother, then retire to his study, where I heard the scraping of paper and books being opened and closed until the small hours of the morning.

After sunrise, I was nibbling on a roll at the table with my brother and sister, watching his every move with keen interest, and entirely forgetting how to act normal.

"Why are you eating like that?" my sister asked me, her nose wrinkled in confusion.

I didn't reply to her. I only kept watching my father, until he turned to me, catching me off guard.

"You mustn't come in to work today," Father told me over breakfast. He hadn't eaten. He had just thrown on his cloak, tucking that strange necklace inside, his hand lingering on it for a moment.

"Oh? Why not?"

"We are – we are still managing a situation. Nothing for you to worry about." His words came out quickly, like he couldn't say them fast enough in his rush to be off.

He left, closing the door a little too hard on his way out. I stared at the closed door for a long while, until my brother waved a hand in front of my face to catch my attention.

While I waited in line at the baker's later in the morning, waiting to buy a loaf of bread, a messenger tapped me on my shoulder and slipped me a piece of paper.

We're meeting her today. Don't forget. At noon.
Across town, by the old church. —F

Excitement, and a little bit of trepidation, kindled to life. It was time to see our strange deal through, to see whether it had been worth it. As I left the bakery, I stuck the note into the flame of a candle resting atop a table, and then dropped it, burning, into the street.

I prepared to leave long before it was time, lacing up my tall boots slowly and carefully. I commonly wore a skirt over a pair of tights, but today I tucked a pair of too-large trousers into my boots and slipped into a brown coat with ruffled shoulders. My mother never wore it any more, so I'd made it mine. Everything was a little too big, but I wanted a disguise, of sorts. It was silly, probably, but it made me feel better.

I left home close to noon. The city was its usual self; whatever panic the Guild was in, it had not made an impression on the outside world. The streets were still full and alive, chatter rose up as one great, humming noise, taverns still held people, and life carried on. I passed close to the Guild on my walk, eyeing its towering form and wondering what sort of things were happening inside. Did any of them suspect, yet, that it had been me?

I shivered.

The old church Feodor had mentioned was decrepit now. It hadn't been used in recent memory. A newer one had been built a few decades ago, and there had always been talk of what to do with the old one, but time had dragged on and stones had started to fall, and no one had bothered to fix it.

Now it was home to birds and whatever other little creatures could find their way inside. You could see its old bell tower a few streets before you reached it, standing broken and angled in the sky. I always worried that if I stood directly underneath it, it would choose that moment to fall.

"Siya!"

Feodor caught up to me just before I reached the church. My name sounded different when it came from his mouth, like it didn't belong to me.

Tiredness made his eyes dark, his face a bit gaunt, but he still offered a small smile. There was something different between us now. Something familiar.

"They know," I said, gesturing behind me in the direction of the Guild. "They know Farod is missing."

"I know."

Of course he did. "My father isn't himself. He was up all night doing gods know what. He told me not to come in today."

"As did mine. They told all the Charges to stay home. Seems like they only want the Officials and the Magisters around."

"What do you think they're doing?"

Feodor shrugged, looking all around us. His hands were shoved into the pocket of his red coat, and his hair was wilder than usual. "Trying to find out where he's gone, using magic, if they can. Trying to figure out who might have set him free. Only a select few would have known about his presence there. They'll be tearing each other apart from within, all pointing fingers."

"Can they trace his release back to you? Through magic?"

"Unlikely, and not quickly. I shielded the incantation, so it's harder to trace. It leaves nothing behind. No echoes.

Most Charges wouldn't have learned how to do that yet, but… Like I've said before, I have a lot of spare time." He smiled sheepishly.

"I feel bad. Do you?"

He looked at me for a moment. "We did what we did. What's done is done—" A horrid sound silenced him, close by, but out of sight. A scream, a muffled one, and it ended quickly. There was a chance I had imagined it.

Feodor spun around. I pointed a finger to an alley across the street.

"I think it came from there." The quiet that followed the scream was worse than the scream itself.

We crept across the street, with me trying to outpace Feodor. Whatever sight awaited us, I wanted to see it first.

When we peered around the corner, a scream choked up in my own throat. Farod stood in the alley, his hand around the throat of a man whose purple robes of an Official peeked out from a worn brown cloak. Farod was bathed in a strange yellow light, and he breathed in deeply as the man in his grasp grew paler and paler. The air smelled of something burning, and a moment later, the light shrank in on itself until it vanished.

Farod wasn't skeletal any more.

His face had shifted somehow, and he was more filled out than before; he had colour in his cheeks. He carried himself more gracefully, and his hair had been pulled back tightly and tied. If it weren't for the same boots and coat as when I had first seen him in the Sanctum, I could so easily believe it was someone else entirely. He looked like a man now. A man like the one whose body he now dropped unceremoniously on to the street.

I slapped a hand over my mouth to keep the flood of angry words inside, and stepped back around the corner, pressing my back up against the wall of a building. *Breathe. Just breathe.* Beside me, Feodor cursed through his teeth.

"Is something the matter?" Viveka's voice trickled down the street.

I pushed away from the wall and faced her. "Look," I said. Fury burned through the fear. "Look at what your *lover* has done."

She glanced down the alley, dropping her hood to her shoulders. "Farod!" she called, and for a very small moment, I realized I didn't want Viveka ever to be angry at me.

Farod whirled in her direction.

"Leave him. *Now.*" Farod glanced back down, then stepped away.

"You said you would watch him," Feodor breathed. "We trusted you."

"I can't watch him every moment of the day," Viveka answered, turning back around to face us. "That's impractical. Though I am sorry. I take no joy in the loss of innocent lives. However, there is something to be said for holding up my end of our deal, which is what I have come here to do."

109

I tried not to look at the body, but my eyes kept finding their way there. He had been alive only moments ago. Living. Breathing. Now he was nothing more than a heap of robes on the cobblestones. Still. Lifeless.

Was the piece of the map worth this? The question bobbed to the surface, no matter how many times I tried to force it back down.

Farod moved to stand behind Viveka, watching us with sharp eyes. Watching Feodor, mostly.

"We cannot talk here," Viveka told us, and she turned to walk towards the old church. "Come with me."

"No one is meant to go in there," I told her stiffly.

"Oh?" she said, glancing at me over her shoulder. "I didn't realize you cared about the rules." She pulled open the creaking door and walked inside.

Feodor and I followed her in. Inside was little better than the outside – piles of rubble, broken windows strung with cobwebs, old wooden chairs. Pinpricks of light filtered in through the vines that had grown over to protect the ceiling, giving the entire place the unwelcome feeling of a dungeon.

I'd had quite enough of dungeons for one week.

Farod slunk in behind us, bringing a chill as he moved gracefully passed Feodor and me to stand behind Viveka.

"Where is the map?" I asked, anxious to leave as soon as may be.

"I didn't bring it with me, of course," Viveka replied, smiling.

"You promised us the map." Feodor's voice was just shy of a shout, anger simmering beneath his veneer of politeness.

"I said I would tell you where to find it," Viveka said evenly. "So I will. You will find it," she said, dropping her voice into a whisper, "in the possession of Queen Hana."

I laughed, far too loudly. Nervously. Surely this was a joke.

"The queen," Feodor said. "The piece of map is in the possession of the queen?"

"The queen, yes. She has had it for some time now, keeping it a secret from the Guild."

"Why – and forgive me for my ignorance here," I said, "would the queen have a piece of the map, and not use it to save the city?"

"That," Viveka said, "I don't know. You would need to ask her for yourself."

"I don't believe you," I said. Farod hissed softly.

"I hardly care," Viveka replied with a shrug. "I said I would tell you what I knew, and I've done that. I thank you for your part in freeing Farod. Your kindness will not soon be forgotten."

"It doesn't make sense," Feodor said quietly. "Queen Hana would have worked with the Guild. She would have saved Shard by now. It… It doesn't make sense."

"Then look into it," Viveka said.

"How do you even know this?" I asked. "I pride myself as being a busybody, and yet this is the first I've ever heard of it. I'm sure you can forgive my scepticism."

"I told you before," Viveka said. "I deal in secrets and knowledge. It takes a lot of time and work, and it rarely amounts to anything, so I save up what I hear and use it for what I need most. The city has secrets and answers, if you know how to listen. I learned that a long time ago." She shrugged. "You can believe me or not. I kept my part of the bargain."

And before either of us could speak again, she left the church, with Farod close behind her.

It was a long walk from the church back home. We walked in silence, and I realized after a while that we were taking the route that would lead us past the palace.

I rarely had reason to draw near to it, and even when I did, I rarely looked up at it, because I'd seen it too many times for it to inspire much interest. But now, as its white walls rose up high overhead, spires reaching into the invisible sky, I couldn't look away. The Snowfall Palace, as it was known. Beautiful, in a cold and uninviting way.

Queen Hana, daughter of Queen Ulyana, who had been in power when the city was cursed, had not emerged in years. In the aftermath of what Baba Yaga had done, the city had turned to the crown, hoping that Ulyana would work with the Guild to find a way to save it. Instead, she had disappeared behind the towering walls and left us all alone, as had her daughter. Turned their backs on the city when it needed them the most.

Or so everyone said. So the Guild had said, specifically.

Queen Hana was now only the queen of the city. Back in Sarsova, there had been a king in Tryvinski, but Hana's mother, Ulyana, had ruled Shard, working with the Guild to practise and protect map magic, and to keep the dreygas far away. All the things the true king had little time or patience to deal with. Affairs of magic have a way of getting messy.

"I've never looked at it for so long," I said, as we stared up at the wall that stood across a canal and up a grassy slope. A grand, wide avenue led up to the gates – always closed. Above the wall that encircled it, a thousand towers and turrets rose up, watching over the city below, intricate as though carved from snow itself.

I knew little of the queen, or what she even looked like. Her mother had been a coward who had turned away in the city's time of need. She had sealed herself away in her sprawling palace, while below, Shard suffered in a hundred thousand ways. Trade had ceased. Food that was once grown outside in the wide fields of Sarsova had been cut off.

We knew Hana was now the queen, but little else. They were as closed off from us as we were from the world.

"I have," Feodor replied, interrupting my thoughts. "I used to come here often when I was younger." He gave me an embarrassed smile. "I wondered about her. What sort of person she might be, beyond the stories."

"She turned her back on us," I told him, lightly kicking a loose cobblestone a few times. "Or so we've been told."

Feodor shrugged. "If Viveka is right, and the queen has the final piece of the map, getting it will be impossible. No one has gone in or out of the palace in decades, not even the Guild, and I have reason to believe they have tried, using map magic."

I groaned. "I wish something could be easy, just once," I said.

"If it was easy, it would have been done by now," Feodor told me. He grinned. "Still, it's worth a try, isn't it? We've come this far."

I found myself smiling back at him before catching myself. It hadn't been so long ago that I had thought him as pompous and useless as Semyon.

"Yes," I said. "We've come this far. What's a bit further, after all?"

8

I woke feeling tired, and a little unpredictable. A night of thinking and wondering if Farod had murdered anyone else had left me drained.

I had barely set foot in the kitchen when Father appeared.

"You are not to come to the Guild today," he said. There were lines on his face that hadn't been there before.

"Again? Why not?" I asked.

He didn't even come up with an excuse this time. "Because I said so."

I watched from across the room as he pulled on his Magister robes, while Mother stood close by, silently. She sensed his mood. Kept silent and offered him the things he might need, sympathy haunting her features. She was always so good. So well intentioned and eager to help. Sometimes I wondered if she could sense the shadows that sometimes followed my father. The sense of *something* that filled the space he left behind. If she did, she never said so.

Did she know what had happened? Had Father told her anything? How many Guild secrets did he share with her?

Mother very rarely used her magic. She was an honorary Guild member, because of being married to my father, but she had never pursued it to the same degree as him.

When he was ready to leave, I crossed the room quickly and followed him outside.

"Father," I said as he stepped out of the door. He spun, his face flushing with annoyance. "I have a question."

"I do hope it's a quick one."

"It is. I – I heard a rumour in the city, that—" I cleared my throat, suddenly nervous. "I heard a rumour that the queen has a piece of the map. I thought, perhaps, you might know more."

Something – *something*, slid across his features. A touch of surprise. Maybe delight. It made me feel a bit sick. He hadn't known this, that much was clear, and suddenly I knew I had made a mistake in telling him.

"Where did you hear that?" he asked simply. His hand reached into his robes to clutch something near his chest.

"In a shop, collecting something for Mother. I overheard people talking. I thought – well, it couldn't be true, could it?"

He looked at me, thinking. I studied every inch of his face.

"It's interesting," he said under his breath. "Very interesting."

As I watched him, standing there in his black robes, his dark hair pulled back into a knot behind his head, something cold slithered between my bones. My father, I realized suddenly, was frightening.

I took an inadvertent step back.

"Did you hear any more. Anything at all?" he asked hungrily.

I shook my head. "That was all. I'm sorry."

Father tapped one foot on the ground a few times, thoughtfully. "Thank you for mentioning it, Siya. Leave it with me."

I stared after him. He was my father. *My father.* I trusted him. Believed in him. Had never had reason to doubt him.

But something was different. Something that didn't feel like the man I knew.

"I'm off for a walk," I called to my mother. The house felt too small and close.

"Take your brother," Mother called from upstairs. "He's been asking for a walk."

"Must I?" I asked as Stepan barrelled towards me.

"Siya!" Mother chided from the tops of the stairs. "Yes, you absolutely must."

He yanked his cloak from the hanger as I opened the door.

Seasons weren't the same since the city had been cursed. We had no real sky, no snow, no rain, but the air grew warm and cold as the seasons changed in Sarsova, and the length of the days continued to change. In a way it was almost worse than nothing changing at all, so close to how things had once been, and yet so far.

Still, I liked to imagine it was snowing on the cold days. If I shut my eyes and concentrated, I could feel the flakes landing on my skin, smell the coldness they brought to the air. Like I had read about in stories. One day, it would be my turn to feel it. My turn to see snow and rain and stars.

Now Sarsova was falling into winter, and the air grew colder day by day.

"Mother says you aren't around enough," Stepan said as we began walking in the direction of a bakery I liked.

"The Guild keeps me busy," I said.

"She thinks you'll end up like Father."

My steps faltered for a moment. "How?"

Stepan shrugged, kicking a stone and sending it skittering away. "I don't know. Too busy. Gone all the time."

"That won't happen."

"What if it already has?"

"Hush, Stepan." I used my sternest warning voice. The thought of turning into my father, after our conversation that morning, chilled me to the bone. "And I think you forget: I have no magic. You're more likely to end up like him than I am."

118

"I get to be a Charge next year," Stepan said with an excited skip, easily distracted from his train of thought. "I will finally be thirteen."

"I know how old you are."

"Then you'll see me more, because I'll always be at the Guild."

"I don't see Charges all that much. I rarely even see Father." *And if you wind up like Semyon I'll lock you in the Sanctum*, I very nearly added.

"I'll make sure you get to see me." He said it like his company was a treat he would bestow on me as often as he could – which would be sweet, if I wasn't so distracted.

"If you say so." We walked in silence for a moment. "It isn't always just fun at the Guild, though," I told him. "It's important that you know that."

"But it's *sometimes* fun."

"Sure, sometimes. But it's hard work, and it takes lots of practice, and sometimes you'll want to give up or think it's impossible. Someone else will be better at it than you, and you'll feel discouraged. Magic is hard work, Stepan."

"How would you know?"

I ground my teeth together. "Because I work at the Guild. I know a good deal more about it than you do."

"Don't do that thing you do, Siya."

"What thing?"

"That thing where you make everything sound dull or terrible. It can't be as bad as all that."

"I don't do that," I told him.

"You do."

"Fine, then think what you want. It won't matter to me."

I retreated into my own thoughts – of Farod and Father and that coldness I had felt while talking to him – as Stepan carried on chatting away about magic and the Guild and his excitement at becoming a Charge as we wound through the city. I led us on a longer route than necessary to take up more time, and he didn't seem to notice. All that awaited me back at home was endless wondering and thinking and worrying. And a little bit of daydreaming about someone with brown hair and a red coat.

Lines of terraced stone buildings stretched away on either side of us. I tore my mind away from worrying and tried to focus instead on the beautiful city we called home. A few houses bore arched doorways with a grand gold knocker, or a handle shaped like a dragon breathing fire. The people in those houses had money.

I used to walk along this street as a child, after reading stories of the old days, when the city was not adrift, because it felt as close as I could get to seeing bits of those stories with my own eyes. Once or twice when my mother or father weren't looking, I had lifted a heavy gold knocker and let it go. I would dart away before anyone could come to the door, but they were too pretty to leave alone.

"Here we are," I said as I spotted the baker's sign with the painted loaf of bread ahead of us.

As I opened the door, a fragmented sentence reached me. "...the queen! I can't believe it."

I shut the door quickly.

"Siya?" Stepan said, staring. "What's wrong?"

"Nothing," I said, my heart pounding. "We're just going to wait until it empties a bit. There are too many people inside. Here, get some of those herbs, would you?" I handed him some coins and pushed him towards a cart selling fresh herbs.

Then I stepped back to the bakery.

Inside the bakery, two Magisters were standing by an open window, whispering to each other. I closed my eyes and strained to listen, grasping for any fragments that might reach me.

"...from his daughter ... quite upsetting..."

"...never thought she..."

"...Hana..."

One of the Magisters glanced towards the window and I dived out of sight. *Had they seen me?*

I climbed to my feet as my brother approached, pointing to a bakery further along the street. "Let's go to that one," I said.

I had only told my father about the queen this morning. News of the rumour had already spread amongst the Guild, rattled them, even. They weren't happy that there might be another piece of map, in the queen's possession. They were worried.

But why? Why didn't they want the map found, and Shard restored to Sarsova?

And then a tiny, violent voice deep within me asked, *What will you do to stop them?*

A shudder rocked my body as we made our way up the street.

We arrived home at the same time as a delivery boy, who handed me a note.

> *Meet me at the south-east tower near the old gates*
> *at noon, if you fancy a climb. —F*

"Who was that from?" Mother asked curiously, taking the shopping from me.

"Just a friend from the Guild," I told her, shoving it into my pocket. It was close on noon now. "Suggesting a walk."

"Hmm." I think she would have pressed me on it further, but my brother and sister began shouting at one another, and she turned away.

The south-east tower was one of four that enclosed the city, once offering sweeping views of Sarsova. It had been the home of guards and the like, a beacon of safety and security for all in the city. Now, the towers sat abandoned and unused.

We had liked to visit them as children, just to climb the winding stone staircases and pretend we could see vast forests and distant mountains below. The last time I had been here was with my brother a year ago, and the view of sheer *nothing*, instead of wild fields and shadowed forests, had been too sad to bear.

Feodor stood outside the door to the tower, with his hands in his pockets. He lifted a hand when he saw me and his face softened. As though we were friends.

I didn't have friends any more – I preferred it that way. It was easier. Easier and less painful than facing sympathetic conversations about how I had no magic.

"I wasn't certain you'd come," he said, brushing hair from his eyes with his fingertips. His face softened as I approached. "Have you been here before?" he asked as we passed through the doors of the tower.

"When I was a kid," I said. "It's not much of a view."

"That depends."

"On what?"

He smiled. "I don't know. On how hard you can imagine a view below you. On … on who you're with." I felt his eyes on me as I looked away.

"After you," he said, gesturing to the stairs. Only one person could reasonably fit at a time. I began the climb, brushing my hand along the stone wall for support as we went.

"How has your father been?"

The question caught me off guard. "Distracted. Angry, even." I wasn't sure whether to tell him about my slip-up.

"As has mine."

I took a deep breath. "I think I did something I shouldn't have done. I – I told him I'd heard a rumour that the queen had a piece of the map."

His steps slowed, then stopped. "Why?"

For a moment, I didn't answer. Why *had* I said anything to my father? "I – I don't know," I said honestly. "I think I wanted to see his reaction. Find out if he knew about it. He didn't, as it turns out."

He was silent.

"What?" I asked.

"I'm wondering whether that was the right thing to do."

"Well, stop wondering," I told him angrily. "It's done. I did it. As far as I can tell, there aren't any rules any more, and nothing makes sense. Whatever book of right and wrong we've been following seems to have been torn up and tossed away. Until a few days ago, I trusted my father. I trusted the Guild. Now I – I don't know any more." I realized I was speaking more to myself than to Feodor, but it felt good to get it all out.

"I know," he said. "Come on. We need to decide what to do next."

Something about the *we* made my heart skip a beat, but I was still angry, so I just turned and carried on climbing.

I remembered from my previous visits to the tower that it was always about halfway up when my legs started to throb, but there was also a window at that point to stop and take in what was once a view. The window faced east, so you couldn't see the city from this side, and it would once have looked out over the land beyond the city walls. A small, makeshift bench had been carved into the stone window frame, allowing a brief rest before finishing the climb. I took it before Feodor could offer it to me.

"What do you see?" he asked, leaning a shoulder against the edge of the window and nodding towards the world outside.

I stared out of the window. The simple answer would be: *I see a brown-grey blur that gives the impression of movement from time to time, but never anything distinct. Not a single tree, or a rock, or shadow.*

But that was the thing about a view that didn't exist: you could create whichever one you needed most.

"A river," I told him, "winding through a great forest. The treetops are sprinkled with snow, and there is more coming. A hart drinks from a pool by the river, and there's a small house tucked away in the woods, with smoke curling from the chimney."

"Is that your house?" Feodor asked.

I shrugged. "It might as well be. I'd like for it to be."

He nodded. "I can see it."

"Don't get too comfortable," I said wickedly. "Only the magicless are allowed inside."

"That doesn't seem fair."

"Doesn't it? Everything else in this city exists for the

magical. We might as well have our own secret places." I had enjoyed imagining the river and the small house, but now I felt cold and empty.

"What do you see?" I asked him.

He thought for a moment, resting his head against the wall and staring out of the window. His thick, dark hair was getting long; it fell in his eyes. "I see another city," he said softly. "Tryvinski, I think, with colourful buildings and towers against the sky. Old libraries and churches to wander, a view of the king's palace impossible to escape no matter which street you're on. New buildings and history to explore and discover, outside of Shard. New streets to get lost in. I think that's what I want, more than anything. Something new. These hundred thousand streets in Shard are old now."

I looked away from him, and back to the window.

I imagined the city he saw, bright and vivid and new to us, but old in every other way. Imagined the streets of a city so old it would take a lifetime to skim the surface of its secrets.

"I want to see something beautiful and distant," I told him. "A fair and faraway land that lives in books. I want to see something new every day."

Feodor sighed, deeply. "I think, perhaps, that we ought to speak to the queen in that case. How else will we save the city?"

"As if you can just speak to the queen," I said heavily. "You can't get into the palace, and she never comes out."

126

"I'm sure we'll find a way," he said, and the confidence in his voice warmed me. "Shall we?" He pointed to the stairwell again, so I slipped down from the window to carry on climbing.

"If the Guild finds Farod," I said, "he may tell them it was us who let him go."

"He might."

"What do you suppose they would do to us?"

Feodor shook his head. "It's better not to wonder about those things. One hour, one day at a time, I think."

That didn't make me feel any better. "What was it like growing up as the son of the next Elder?" I said, to change the subject.

Feodor laughed. "Lonely," he said simply. "I rarely see him. I might as well live alone."

"I'm sorry for that," I told him, because I didn't know what else to say. I knew what it was like to be lonely.

"It is what it is. He is a driven man. Driven men never have enough time." We were silent for a moment. "You have brothers and sisters, don't you?" he asked. "What is that like?"

"They're nice enough," I said. "But ... well, they both have magic, and I don't."

"Ah."

I had never told anyone how it felt being the only one in a family without magic. It was like living in the same house with people, but always being separated by glass. Always something that kept me on the outside looking in.

"When did you find out?" Feodor asked. "That you didn't have magic."

"I don't remember, really. I was very young. I think it just sort of dawned on me one day, that I was missing something my father thought I had. I didn't realize what that meant until I was older."

"How did your father take it?"

I stared at the ground as we climbed, remembering the curious, hungry expression on my father's face that morning. "He was disappointed," I said. "He tried not to show it, but I could tell. You overhear things."

"I'm sorry." He touched my arm, a small show of kindness, but I carried on climbing. Pity wouldn't give me magic. Pity did nothing.

The stairs at last ended and we emerged into the breeze and dizzying heights of the top. I paused for a moment to lean against a post and catch my breath.

The top of the tower was open to the air, with a circular, peaked roof overhead to keep out the rain. On the left lay the city, sprawling and seeming never to end. On the other sat the haze that encircled us as the city wandered and roved about Sarsova. Trapped in whatever plane Baba Yaga had sent it to.

"You forget how beautiful it is," Feodor said, resting both hands on the waist-height wall surrounding us.

"You do," I replied, my breath settling. I pointed towards the round building, standing above the others. "There's the Guild."

128

"It looks small from here," Feodor said. "You can almost believe the things that happened this week never happened at all. Just a story."

"Almost." *But not quite*, I thought. A dreyga, kept prisoner. A scrap of map that wasn't meant to exist. Secrets upon secrets, buried deep.

"The piece of the map," I whispered, even though we were alone. "Do you still have it?"

He nodded. "It's safe. At home. Away from my father."

I stared at the Guild again."

"I've been ... meaning to ask," I ventured after a long moment. "Since, you know, you're so *magical*. How do the dreygas actually kill? What ... what happens?"

Sorrow gathered in his eyes. "They aren't built like we are," Feodor said. "They have something that draws in magic and holds on to it. And if they feed on you... Magic isn't just something you have, it is a *part* of you. An essential part, like your blood or your heart. When it's ripped away, there is too much damage to heal."

I nodded, thinking. "When he ... killed that man," I said, "I thought that afterwards, Farod looked like him, a bit."

Feodor nodded. "Magic is our identity, and when the dreygas kill, it becomes theirs. It fades over time as their magic is used up."

I winced. "Does it hurt?"

· "Yes," he told me flatly. "Or so I'm told."

129

I shivered again. The thought made me feel sick.

"Well, we're alone up here," Feodor said. "I suppose we ought to discuss how we're going to pay a visit to the queen."

"It's impossible," I said. "There's no way in." I smoothed down my shirt, working through my feelings about the words *alone up here*.

He nodded. "Yes, as you say, that will be our biggest difficulty." He looked at the distant palace, thinking, giving me time to study his profile for a few silent moments. "The queen has secured herself in the palace using map magic that even the Guild has not been able to get through. Granted, they may not have tried very hard. They had no reason to."

"They have a reason to try now."

"That's why we have to move fast."

"If they haven't managed to get in, how will we?"

"Magic," he answered. "That's my department. But I need you to find out the layout of the palace and the gardens."

"I have no magic, remember?" I said coldly.

"I don't mean map magic," he told me softly. "I just mean looking at actual maps. Sometimes the old-fashioned ways are best."

"All right," I said. I loved maps – actual maps, that, like me, bore no magic, but held useful information. "Best to avoid the Atheneum for a while, though. I can visit the city's library and see what's there."

Feodor smiled. "Good plan. I'll poke around as well. My father has a small library in our house. He might have something useful in there. Tomorrow – meet back in the gardens, in the evening?"

I nodded, feeling an odd excitement rising in me, warring with the fear. I saw the same reflected in his eyes. We held each other's gaze for a long moment, and then I looked away, unnerved by the intensity of it.

Rested from our climb, we began the easier descent back through the tower and to the ground below.

Feodor walked with me partway home. We chatted about nothing important, pointing out things we had been able to see from the tower, and admiring treats that sat in bakery windows. It felt easy to imagine that nothing had happened. That nothing had changed.

As we passed an alleyway, almost too narrow to walk down without having to turn sideways, I was sure I heard something, a hissing sound, and I stopped and stared into the shadows – but there was nothing there. I was imagining things – Farod on the prowl, talons creeping round corners, orange eyes glowing from the shadows.

Feodor caught my elbow. "Did you hear that?" he whispered.

Through the door of a tavern beside us, loud voices emanated, fragmented as people talked over one another.

"...not what I heard. I heard she's had it for quite some time..."

"…you hear a lot of things. We can't always believe…"

"…but why would she keep it all these years?"

"…say we all just storm up there to ask. She can't turn all of us away."

I stared at Feodor, my heart thudding in my chest. "I told one person," I whispered. "Just one person."

He nodded slowly, his eyes narrowing. "I think he might have told a few more."

9

Twilight was setting in as I made my way through the streets, blanketed in a lavender darkness that crept silently into my bones. The city was still alive and breathing for the day, though doors were shutting and streets were emptying the further along I went.

The Library of Shard was far less grand and lofty than the Guild's Atheneum, but it still held more books than anyone could read in a lifetime, and the rooms still smelled of dust and stories.

The librarian at the front informed me he would be closing in half an hour, so I slipped quickly through the shelves and between stacks of books that littered the floor, my head tilted sideways to read the titles. *What was I even looking for?* Suddenly Feodor's suggestion that I read up on the palace and its layout felt like a task designed to make me feel as though I had something to do. A way to occupy a child.

Framed on a wall, hanging above a dusty hearth that never housed a fire, hung a detailed map of the city, from the sweeping palace, to the Guild, to the intricate streets like threads in a tapestry, all criss-crossing and winding together. I brushed my fingertips over the glass casing, reminded for the second time today of how beautiful the city could be. I could see why there was magic in maps, such beauty and fine detail trapped in something as innocuous as paper.

Maps like these could be read by anyone. Magical. Magicless. And yet ... there was almost a magic in that. The magic of nondescript things. Like me.

I trailed my fingers over the shelves, alighting on a book I had loved as a child. *How the City Came to Wander* – a history of the city and the curse, which included the poem of Nedda and letters from the Guild when Shard was banished. It stood alone between two bookends shaped like mountains. I lifted it gently, and opened it.

The first few pages were taken up with maps of Sarsova, marking where the city had once sat by the great River Sarshk, large enough for boats to carry goods in from the distant sea. From where the city sat, far away to the north, the Bleaks would have just been visible, shrouding the horizon like an encroaching darkness.

The places between the city and the mountains, the wide forests and sweeping hills and bare valleys, were rich with fables and myths. Shaggy-haired forest giants who looked like trees. A sword seen only in the valley on foggy mornings, wielded by no one but always ready for bloodshed.

I sighed dreamily and closed the book. If I had to dig a tunnel with my fingernails to get us into the palace then I would do so, if it meant that I could one day lay eyes on the world myself.

On another shelf, a title seemed to whisper my name. I hesitated, wondering if I was brave enough to pick it up.

Origins of the Dreygas.

Before I could lose my nerve, I slipped the book from the shelf. Dust swirled into the air when I did so – clearly, it was not the read of choice for the library's patrons. I flipped to a random page and scanned the paragraphs.

But how to distinguish between man or monster? While this may seem difficult at first, they make themselves known once you learn their secrets. Learn which parts of them parade as man, and which as magic-eating devils.

If I, as the writer, could impart one notion to the reader that I hope would stay with them for ever, it is this: the roots of the dreygas are, and always will be, human. They *are* human, in almost every sense of the word. Humans who eat and subsist solely on magic. Humans who can think of nothing else.

What separates them from us, however, is that although they can consume magic without end, they can never *use* magic. It will fill them up and burn away and leave them hungrier for more. Starved for it. They may act the part of human once fed, but that too will soon burn away, leaving the beast behind.

I clapped the book shut and stuck it back on the shelf. Maybe not having magic wasn't so bad, if it kept you safe from those monsters.

Maybe.

I heard a soft noise that I recognized as the library doors opening. A slight breeze ruffled my hair, followed by the sound of the library doors closing again.

Instinctively, I shrank behind a stack of books and peered towards the front of the library – and a cold hand wrapped around my heart.

Two Magisters stood facing the librarian, speaking in hushed tones. A particular darkness had entered the room behind them, like the rotten breath of something wicked rushing in their wake.

I held my breath to hear better.

"You have magic, do you not?" one of the Magisters asked. He was leaning towards the librarian, both hands planted on the desk.

"I – well, yes, I do. But I don't use it. I'm not a member of the Guild or anything like that. I like books, you see. Books are my kind of magic."

The Magister held up his hand for silence. "You've been asked to come with us." He motioned for the man to rise. The other Magister stood silently, his hands folded, face nearly hidden beneath his hood.

I gripped a shelf to steady my trembling hands.

"Why?" the librarian said, standing and peering into the Magister's face. "I haven't done anything wrong. I think it's time for you to leave. I was just about to lock up."

"If we have to take you by another means, I promise you will like it far less," said the Magister impatiently. Meanwhile, the other had drawn a parchment from his pocket and had begun to chant something.

"I've heard about this," said the librarian, panic in his voice. "About folk from the city going missing. Heard the Guild had something to do with it. Can't you at least tell me where you're taking me? Or why?"

The Magister behind him only jerked his head towards the door. "We're leaving. Now."

"May I at least lock the doors?" the librarian asked, holding out his keys, his voice quiet now, resigned.

"There's nothing in here of worth," the Magister said, taking the librarian by the shoulders and pushing him towards the door. The keys fell to the floor.

The librarian turned as he was dragged out, and

his eyes met mine as I cowered in the darkness of the shelves. I drew back further, terrified for a moment that he would alert them to my presence. That I too would be dragged away to the Guild for reasons that remained a mystery.

But instead the librarian darted his eyes to the floor, where I saw that he had dropped his keys. He looked at me once more, his expression pleading, before he was shoved out of the room.

The Magister opened the door. It no longer led into the city, but a dark, low hallway that must be somewhere in the Guild. They pushed the man through the door, pulled it closed behind them, and all was silent.

Several long moments stretched away in silence. My breath was ragged; my heart was thunder. Where were they taking him? *Why?* I gripped the edge of a bookshelf until my nail dug into the wood.

Slowly, I crept out from behind the stacks and shelves of books and padded carefully towards the keys. I remembered the man's words.

I like books, you see. Books are my kind of magic.

The librarian had left the keys behind so that I might lock up that which that mattered most to him in the world: his books. There were stacks of them on his desk, some bookmarked halfway through as if he spent his days doing nothing but reading. A cold cup of tea sat beside them, echoes of a mundane day that had taken a wicked turn.

A cold sweat ran down my back, despite the warm room. Where were they taking him? *Why?*

I slowly opened the library doors and peered out. Whatever doorway they had mapped to some other hidden location was gone, leaving nothing but the normal city streets outside. Before I left, I turned back to the shelves and quickly found a book on the palace, tearing out an old map of the gardens and grounds and folding it into my pocket. Then I turned the key in the lock until it clicked softly, and I slipped towards home.

Father came home late again that night.

I was still awake, lying in my bed and staring at the ceiling when I heard his key in the lock. It took everything in me not to go to him. Had he spread the rumour about the queen throughout the city? Why? Did the Guild wish for the city to hate the queen? Where had they taken the librarian? *Why? Why? Why?*

But I didn't dare. I had never really felt close to my father, but now I was afraid of him.

And there was the librarian. The fear in his eyes as he was led through the magical door wouldn't leave me.

I covered my face with my hands in the dark, as Father went to bed. But sleep refused to come.

"You may come in to work today," Father said to me in the morning. He looked tired but composed.

"Oh?" I said, putting down my bread and trying not to look surprised.

"Yes," he said simply, pulling on his cloak. "There is work to be done."

I watched him leave the house. Something was different today. Something had changed. I tried to imagine all the things it might be – *they had found the map they had captured the dreyga* – but the creeping unease only grew worse, and I couldn't place why.

I got ready slowly and left the house, wondering all the while. Perhaps things were returning to normal. Perhaps no one would ever know about what I'd done. Perhaps the Guild had captured Farod again, and that was the end of the matter.

If this was all over, then Feodor and I would no longer need to spend time together. There would be no more *we*. I ran a hand over my damp forehead, sweat clinging to my skin as the Guild came into view. Nothing had changed. Not a stone out of place. Almost as if I had awoken today from a bad dream.

Which was what I had wanted. Wasn't it? The large doors groaned as I entered. I stopped dead in the foyer.

My Father, Official Fredek, Ermolai and four or five other Magisters and Officials stood in a half circle inside, all watching me. There was no one else in the area.

They were waiting for me.

Fear nearly blinded me. I kept one hand on the door handle for support.

"Good morning!" I said lightly. "Were you expecting me?"

"We were," my father replied, waving one hand to the stairs. "Please. Join us."

I thought of the librarian, led away by Magisters. They waited politely for me to start walking. As I crossed the foyer with slow steps, they sank into a crescent behind me, blocking off the door. I glanced back to see a line of black and lavender robes fencing me in. Escape was beyond reach.

I ascended the steps slowly. There were other routes out of the Guild, but every time I glanced to the side, a Magister or an Official was seamlessly blocking off a hallway or a staircase that would ultimately lead to an exit. They had thought about this. My knuckles tightened on the banister.

At the top of the stairs – on the floor which the Magisters usually occupied – Feodor sat waiting outside a room with a great table. Officials stood on either side of him, guards in Guild robes. His eyes were cast down.

"What is this?" I asked finally, turning to my father.

"You'll know soon enough," he answered. "We have a few questions."

"Questions?" I repeated. "This seems fairly aggressive, just for a few questions."

"Don't be silly," he told me. A father talking to his ill-behaved daughter. Not a threatening Magister speaking to a suspect. "In you go, Siya," he said, and placed a hand on my back to gently push me into the room with the large table. I met Feodor's eyes as I passed, and he rose to follow us inside – sending me a smile that lit his eyes like fire. Strength flickered inside me.

Until I found Semyon, sitting at the table inside. Then all spark and flame disappeared. His sneer was so large it took up the room.

"Must he be here?" I asked, slumping into the chair opposite him and glaring at him.

"Yes. He must be," Official Fredek said. His voice was heavy. He wasn't enjoying this any more than I was.

Everyone else seated themselves, eyeing me with distrust as my father closed the door. He turned back to face us slowly, his hands lingering on the door as he thought.

"Siya, we have a few questions for you," he said, taking a seat near the head of the table, beside Ermolai, Feodor's father. Feodor sat beside me.

I rubbed my sweaty palms on my lap. "Yes, you mentioned that."

"I have volunteered to ask most of them, as you're my daughter."

I said nothing.

"To put it simply, Siya, a prisoner has gone missing, posing a threat to everyone in the city. We want to know if you might have played a role in his escape."

A *prisoner*. The word made it sound so much simpler than it was. I let surprise spread across my face, filtering into disbelief. "No, oddly enough, I did not. I make it a point of not getting involved in things outside filing and note-taking."

It came out so naturally, I was momentarily alarmed by my fantastic ability to lie so easily. I really ought to remember how good I was at this.

My father's eyes narrowed, studying me. "I know you like to poke around in the Guild, Siya."

"Oh, I do. Without a doubt. The Atheneum is a fascinating place. And *did you know* that it contains over *five million books*? Yarik told me that. Absolutely wild." I sounded so cool and collected.

"Siya."

"*What?*" I dared him to go on. To be honest with me.

"This wasn't just any prisoner."

I leaned forward. "Really, Father? What kind of prisoner was it?"

His eyes darted to the others, as though wondering if he should say it. He cleared his throat. "It was a dreyga."

There it was. A few others in the room shifted uncomfortably. *A dreyga? In the Guild? Who had ever heard of such a thing? How utterly irresponsible.*

I drew in a long breath. "Why ... would the Guild ... have a dreyga?" It was the one question I had been desperate to ask, and it felt like a weight off my chest, once it was out in the air. It suited the moment, though. I sounded truly shocked.

He waved a hand. "He was a … leftover from a long time ago. Before the city was cursed."

"I thought they were all destroyed. Why weren't they?"

"Our reasons are not yours to know, although you may rest easy in the comfort that the things we do are only for the purposes of bettering and furthering magic, the Guild, the city and Sarsova at large."

What of those without magic?

"Holding on to a dreyga feels like the height of irresponsibility. Especially if there was a risk of it getting loose in the city."

"There wasn't a risk of that."

"Then where is it?"

He sighed, pinching the bridge of his nose. "We don't know."

I glanced at Feodor during the quiet moment that followed. He was watching me with an expression I couldn't read.

"Father, why would I know of a dreyga's escape?" I let a bemused smile play across my lips. "Why would I know it was here in the first place? I file papers, Father. I take notes on Charges. I serve the same function as a rug or a stair handle: useful, but in a limited way. How could I have freed a dreyga, of all things? I have no magic, in case you've forgotten." For once, reminding him of such a thing felt like a relief.

· "I haven't forgotten," my father replied simply, as though it was a thought that had plagued him, day in and day out. "But you are sharp. You see things. Remember them. We believe it's possible that you learned of the dreyga's existence and decided to free it."

"Why?"

"Why what?" My father was reaching the end of his patience.

"Why do you believe that?"

"Semyon believes he saw you sneaking into the Sanctum with Feodor."

A chill gripped me, harsh and unrelenting. The sounds we had heard down in the dungeons, when we thought someone was coming. Had Semyon been following us? My gaze settled on his simpering, snake-like form.

"I know what I saw, I'm afraid," he said pompously. "When I learned of the dreyga's escape, I felt compelled to tell the Guild of your presence near the Sanctum that day."

"You're pathetic," I snapped. "Telling lies, just to get their attention."

"Siya," my father said, a warning note in his voice. "Just answer the question."

"*Of course* I did not free a dreyga," I said loudly, exasperated. "I cannot think of a single reason why I would

145

do such an absurd and reckless thing. I would not be *able* to!"

"You have no magic," Semyon told me simply. "It would have posed no threat to you."

"Forgive me," I told him, taking in all the faces around the room that watched me with an unsettling intensity. "But I do not consider myself an expert on the dangers of dreygas."

"You hardly have to be an expert to know that."

"How would I have let it out?" I asked, through my teeth.

"Maybe you didn't," Semyon said. "Feodor could have worked the magic for you."

I snorted. "You think that Feodor, who I barely know, would do that? Why?"

I had the satisfaction of watching Semyon hesitate.

Feodor shifted. "Actually," he said, "I'd like to speak now, if I may."

Everyone was quiet, and my father nodded for him to go on.

"Siya and I *were* in the Sanctum that day," he admitted, looking down at the table.

I stiffened. *What was he thinking?* I gripped the edge of the table as Feodor went on.

"We didn't go far. Just somewhere to offer … a bit of privacy." His cheeks flooded red. He looked wretchedly embarrassed. "You know how it is."

A silence swept across the room. Semyon wrinkled his nose, horrified. "A ... rendezvous? With a *Clerk*?"

It took everything I had not to launch across the table to wring Semyon's neck.

"I know," Feodor said, as though he couldn't believe it himself. "Hence the secrecy. I didn't exactly want anyone to know."

I swallowed, letting my eyes meet his. My own had filled with tears.

He glanced away from me. "Semyon got it wrong. I apologize for breaching the Sanctum. But we are innocent, at least of freeing the dreyga."

My father cleared his throat, clearly uncomfortable.

"Siya, is this true? Is that why you were in the Sanctum?" My father's voice held disgust, and impatience.

I looked at Feodor again. Waited for him to say something. But he stayed quiet. "Yes," I lied coldly. "Semyon jumped to conclusions."

"No," Semyon said flatly. "I know what I saw."

"And I know what I saw on the Charge outing, but you don't see me telling everyone," I snapped.

A few heads turned towards Semyon, who shifted uncomfortably in his seat. "I don't know what you're talking about."

I shrugged. "Feodor was there too."

"Perhaps you would like to enlighten us, Feodor. I'm curious," Official Fredek said.

Feodor nodded. "I believe Siya is referring to Charge Semyon's reckless use of magic in a city bakery while attempting to prove himself more powerful than Baba Yaga." He leaned back in his chair and crossed his arms, mirroring the poised way many of the Magisters sat silently.

All eyes turned to Semyon, whose face had gone pale. "I – that's – it was a mistake," he said under his breath.

Ermolai inhaled deeply, slowly, in a way that made me shiver.

"I recall it quite clearly, as a matter of fact," Feodor replied. "As, I'm sure, will the other Charges who were present on that day."

"Surely, you can see what they are attempting to do," Semyon said to the Magisters and Officials, his voice a mixture of angry and pleading. "They freed a dreyga, and they're getting away with it."

"I think you must know that isn't true," Feodor told him gently. "Siya here has no magic. And I would never think to do something as reckless as freeing a dreyga. But I think there is someone in this room who would. Someone who has done that sort of thing before."

Feodor sat back in his chair, the picture of confidence and ease.

"How dare you?" Semyon hissed. The anger in his eyes scared me. "You might think you can deceive them, but I know the truth. *I know* what I saw. *I know* what you did."

"Feodor, Siya, we will pick this up later," said Ermolai, his tone grave. "Perhaps it's best if you head home."

"You're going to let them just walk out the door?" Semyon cried. "Dreyga-freers? Liars?"

"Of course," Ermolai replied. "They aren't prisoners. And the city is cursed. There is nowhere to run."

There is nowhere to run.

The words hung thick in the air as Feodor and I silently left the room.

I let my feet carry me where they would, silently, without thinking. Down the stairs, across the foyer, through the great doors and out into the brisk air. Down the street, across the square, and then I stopped in a quiet side street where a few children played close by, rolling a wooden ball across the cobblestones.

The fresh air of freedom, away from the Guild and the Magisters and the darkness, smelled sweeter and more beautiful than ever.

"You know I didn't mean it, right?" Feodor asked beside me.

I jumped at his voice, and took a minute to study his face. "Yes. You were just making up a cover story," I said lightly. "It was a good one." That didn't mean it didn't hurt, though. I winced at the memory.

"I just – I had to find a way to make Semyon's accusation seem like nonsense. Something believable." He was looking at me, worried. Why? Why did he care what I – a mere *Clerk* – thought of him?

"Of course. You probably didn't have to be quite so convincing, though. If you feel that way about Clerks, you had a lot of chances to tell me to leave you alone without having to suffer my presence so much." I plucked at a loose thread by the pocket of my cloak.

Feodor stepped closer. "I don't feel that way about Clerks," he said quietly. "Siya, I didn't mean what I said. Are you all right?"

"Yes." I rubbed tears from my eyes. "Or not. I don't know." I ran my hands up and down my arms. "That was all just so awful. I wasn't expecting any of it." I heaved a sob, then calmed down a bit.

"Nor was I."

Feodor leaned his back against a wall of the alley, his head resting against the stone, but his eyes were still on me. "You didn't seem nervous. In fact, you conducted yourself with all the brazen attitude of Semyon on a day he feels particularly conceited."

I shrugged. "They already think I'm worthless," I said, plucking at a loose bit of stone in a wall. "You said it yourself. I'm just a Clerk. Barely. A Clerk-in-training." My voice got quieter with each word I spoke.

"Siya..." The word was impossibly gentle. "Why don't you believe in yourself?"

He was standing so close, our faces were only inches apart. I could see every fleck in his eyes, every line around them. The arch in the middle of his upper lip.

"What is there to believe in?" I asked quietly.

He moved even closer. "I don't understand the question. There is *so much* to believe in. So much strength and ambition and hope bound up in flesh and bone." He rubbed a knuckle gently against my forearm. "I believe in you enough for the both of us. And you know why?"

"Why?" The word escaped in a whisper.

"Because if it wasn't for you, we would still be in the Guild right now, being questioned, imprisoned. Your quick thinking is the reason we are standing here, together."

Deep down I didn't believe him, not really, but he spoke so convincingly that I drank in every syllable like water. But the things he'd said about me, the way he had seemed so embarrassed to be saying them, still stung like a skinned knee.

"It was my vindictive tendencies that freed us," I told him. "I would feed Semyon to Farod and feel nothing."

A deep chuckle rose up from his throat. "Anyway." He took a step back, pushing hair from his face with both palms.

I didn't want to spoil the moment with more dark news, but I had to tell him. "There's something you don't know." I looked up and down the side street, but we were the only souls in sight. "I went to the library last night, like I said I would."

"Learn anything interesting?"

"In a manner of speaking." I swallowed, still picking at

151

the wall. "Two Magisters showed up. I hid. They took the librarian. They asked him if he had magic, and then they mapped the library door back to the Guild and took him away."

Feodor stiffened, his eyes delving deep into mine. "They took him?"

I nodded. "They took him. Gone." I kicked the wall, then regretted it when an ache splintered through my foot.

Feodor turned to stare up the street – towards the Guild, even though it was out of sight. "Devils," Feodor whispered into the chilly air. "All of them."

I said nothing, just waited quietly as the sounds of the city hummed away.

"What do we do?" he said. "We haven't the luxury of time any more. If we are to reach the queen, it must be now. Whatever they hope to achieve cannot be achieved without her piece of the map. We have to beat them to it."

"At dawn, tomorrow," I told him, dropping my voice to barely above a whisper. "If we could sneak into the Sanctum and release a captive dreyga, we can surely find our way into the palace."

"I admire that confidence," Feodor said with a grin. "Let's hope it's not misplaced."

I turned to leave.

"In the gardens?" he called, holding his hair out of his eyes with a fist. "I think a rest, and some food might be needed."

"The gardens," I told him, and turned to go.

A coldness settled into me the moment I was alone. I crossed my arms inside my cloak and walked quickly, head down, winding down back streets and passageways that would bring me home the fastest. For once, I longed for home. Longed for my brother's voice, playing with his toys in the corner. My sister, reading a book nearby, the pages rustling every few moments as she turned them delicately. Mother humming to herself as she went about her day.

All the things that had grown mundane and uninteresting over the years suddenly made me ache with longing. For things to return to normal. That was what I truly wanted. A Shard without dreyga. A Guild that didn't suspect me of anything. A commonplace life.

A hiss jolted me to a stop, and I knew before I saw him that Farod was near.

Anyone else might have discounted it, passing it off as one of the sounds of the city. But I had heard it before.

Ducking around a corner, I peered out slowly, his gangly form towering in a very narrow passageway, almost too small to walk down without having to turn sideways. And in his grasp was a man I didn't know, but who had map parchment partially visible in his cloak pocket.

A silent sob shook me. All the quiet hopes I'd harboured that perhaps the Guild had captured him again, or that Viveka would keep him away from the city streets, evaporated into the air around me. That crumpled man on the ground *would still be alive* if it wasn't for me. If *I* hadn't let Farod go free.

I bit down hard to keep quiet, as Farod choked the last bits of air from the man's lungs and flung him to the ground.

I fled down the street like I was chased by fire.

10

I sat alone in the gardens after another sleepless night, waiting for Feodor and trying to look calm.

Tall order.

I had managed to sneak out of the house before anyone else was awake, in an effort to avoid my father. I didn't know what I might say to him if I saw him – or what he might say to me. Best not to run into each other at all today.

I turned to look up at the palace, lurking overhead like an eye that watched us, always. Unreachable but inescapable. White as ice and snow and as beautiful as any palace in the storybooks. But a symbol of neglect, and a queen who had forsaken us.

At my sides, I curled my hands into fists and released them again. *You wanted to have a less ordinary life, Siya. You begged for it. Longed for it. Dreamed of it.*

My temple throbbed. How much adventure could a person take? How thoroughly could the pillars of the world as we knew it be shaken before we crumbled?

"Siya." Feodor's voice reached me from far away. I turned. "Feodor."

A smile warmed his face. A beautiful smile. He glanced at the palace. "She's a beauty."

Around us, the hum of the city wore on. Louder voices rose above the rest. The occasional clang of a cart. The call of birds in the nearby trees. For a moment, everything felt right. Everything felt as it always had. And for a moment, it was as if nothing had changed.

"I saw Farod again," I told him.

Feodor let out a long breath and rubbed his eyes for a moment. "Ah. What did he say?"

"Oh, we didn't speak. He was busy killing someone." I bit out the words through gritted teeth.

"Oh. Oh *gods*." Feodor turned and walked away from me a few steps, then came back, slowly, staring at nothing. I knew that we were thinking exactly the same thought. *What have we done?*

It was Feodor who broke the silence, shaking his head. "Right. Well, we best get down to business. I think I've found us a way in. There's a canal that runs on to the grounds from the east side of the city. Its entry is blocked by a grate, and likely some amount of magic, but I think I can get us in."

"A grate," I said flatly. "It's too obvious."

He shrugged defensively. "I'm not proud of it, but it's all I could find. I'm hoping anyone who has tried before has been put off by whatever amount of map magic they encountered, and gave up."

I nodded, fighting down panic. Sneaking into the Sanctum through magic was one thing, but breaking into the palace was entirely another. The sudden notion of simply leaving the garden and returning home darted into my mind. Dreaming of something was infinitely harder than doing something, I was learning.

But Shard was worth saving. Shard *deserved* saving.

"Are you frightened?" Feodor said quietly.

"Of course not," I shot back, then drew in a breath. "Yes. Terrified. And don't pretend you're not."

He laughed a little. "No. I'm just as frightened as you are."

"Does that mean we shouldn't do it?"

"No, it means we must. We would be foolish if we weren't afraid. Doing something reckless without fear can hardly be called bravery. Siya—"

Keep saying my name. The words found their way into my mind, suddenly and powerfully.

"—we are in it this far. We can't stop now. Besides" – he grinned at me – "it would be hard for things to get much worse."

"So, we're breaking into the palace. I feel like I'm in a feverish dream." I pressed my hand to my forehead.

"We're not breaking in. We're taking advantage of a weak spot in order to further our cause."

"Mmm," I said, nodding, "or in simpler terms, breaking in."

"Fine, breaking in." He held out his arm. "Shall we?"

I reached for his arm, and then my world went dark.

Something was suddenly thrust over me, cutting off the world. Darkness pressed in, thick cloth cascading over my head and shoulders.

A muffled voice outside my sudden enclosure – Feodor's, or someone else's?

I fought against the cloth, but I was bound too tightly. "Let me go!" I yelled. My feet left the ground for a few sickening seconds, then my body thudded on to what could have been a cart.

We began to move.

Screaming was a waste of time. I could hardly breathe as it was, in my stifling cloth prison. I kept my eyes closed, as though I could have seen anything with them open, and focused only on breathing. One breath, two breaths, three breaths…

The cart rolled along. A horse's hooves clanged along cobbled streets. Distracted from my breathing for a moment, I tried to judge where we might be based on the sounds of the city, but only the sharpness of the hooves and the deep rolling of the cart made it through the cloth.

This was it, then. No more prying questions and game-playing. The Guild had caught up with us, and before long, one of those stuffy, ancient cells in the Sanctum would be mine. I let out a choked sound of frustration.

"Hush," said an unfamiliar voice very close to me. I froze.

Now and then, muffled voices made their way through the cloth. Nothing distinct, just a low hum now and again, in the occasional cadence that reminded me of enchantment incantations. Where *were* they taking us? A hidden way into the Sanctum? A secret door into the dungeons, so we might avoid prying eyes in the Atheneum?

The cart came to a sudden halt. I swallowed.

I was dragged out and set on my feet. I staggered, dizzy, my legs tingling from disuse. A moment later, I was lifted again and propped on a seat that tilted up and down.

"Water," I whispered to myself. "A boat." There were no canals near the Guild. At least not that I could recall. I could sense another body sitting close to mine, occasionally brushing my shoulder. Feodor.

Another incantation started. I couldn't make out the words, but it flowed quietly on, rhythmic, the one speaking it now much closer than before. The boat bobbed along. The air around us smelled charred, like a candle that had just been blown out.

The incantation stopped. I was pulled from the boat, placed back on my feet, and a moment later, the fabric was pulled away.

159

I blinked at our captors, expecting my father or Ermolai or even Fredek. I found only the faces of strangers in chocolate-brown cloaks.

"Who—" I began, but Feodor held up a hand, pointing at something I had not yet seen.

Ornate white walls towered above us. Grand doors carved with white leaves stood tall; five or six grown men stacked atop one another would still find themselves unable to reach the top. Dozens of towers, each unique in their shape and height, rose up into the blurred sky, the flags of Sarsova and the City of Shard waving lightly in the breeze.

"Welcome to the palace," said the voice of one of our captors. He had a deep voice and a pleasant face. Younger than my father, but older than me and Feodor. "Apologies for the manner of your journey."

I turned back to face them. "We would have gone easily, you know. We wanted to break in!"

"The way in is a secret, for Her Majesty's safety." The two cloaked figures walked towards the grand doors.

I met Feodor's gaze, briefly, and mouthed, *Safety?* He shrugged, only barely.

"Hurry up," one of the captors called, clapping his hands twice as the giant doors groaned open. My mouth went dry as we followed them through the doors – and they ground closed behind us.

The palace. We were inside the palace.

This must, *must* be a dream.

Ornate tiles of white and pale blue yawned away before us, in a foyer so large it could swallow ten of my houses with room to spare. A chandelier overhead burned brightly, hung with a hundred candles that all dripped down into great piles of cooled wax on the floor, forming an intricate and haphazard sculpture in the centre of the room. The wax was taller than me, taller, even, than Feodor, with lines and waves that made me think of drifted snow. Hallways ambled away into the far recesses of the palace, and away across the room, a staircase with a gold railing split to climb up to somewhere unseen, in separate directions.

"This way," said the man who led us, motioning to the large staircase that led up and to the right. It reminded me of the one in the Guild, though far more grand and gilded.

I climbed up slowly, running my hand along the gold railing gingerly. If this *was* a dream, it might shatter and dissolve into nothing.

I paused halfway up to take in the foyer below, soaking in the chandelier and the strange wax sculpture and the carved doors, wondering how it could be that the queen lived here and didn't spend every moment standing just here, staring. Admiring such beauty that was *hers*.

"Siya." Feodor called to me from the top of the stairs. I breathed in the view one last time, then ascended the remaining steps quickly.

The top of the grand staircase found us in another white hallway with a floor like the one below, only narrower and with countless windows that were all shrouded by the same rich blue drapes that kept any ounce of light from seeping in. I took in a fistful of the velvet drapes, feeling the rich fabric.

"You mustn't touch that," said our captor from down the hall. "Follow me, please."

I brushed hair from my face, indignant at being rebuked. And why was *every curtain* drawn?

The hallway finally ended at a winding staircase, with a carved white railing that made it look as though miniature drifts of snow were darting off it in every direction.

Up, up, up. The staircase wound on, bringing hope that around each bend I might see the final step, but it carried on climbing ever onwards into the clouds, past the sun, and was certain to drop us amongst the unseeable stars. My breath left me, and I clung to the railing with both hands, pulling myself up one more step, one more step. Though we had passed no windows on our climb, the passageway seemed to be bathed always in a bright white light that washed down from somewhere high above.

And when at last the staircase ended, I tumbled on to the floor and lay very still.

My cheek pressed to the floor, I opened my eyes to see Feodor lying close beside me, out of breath but smiling. Desperate for a rest. He wasn't afraid. If his eyes were any indication, he was enjoying every moment of this. I pushed off from the ground to sit up.

The room was large and round, with four windows that all let in daylight from the world outside. Silhouetted against the brightness stood a woman in a white dress, with white-and-blue-striped sleeves that ran down almost to her fingers. A crown rested on her head, so fine and delicate it seemed certain to be made of frost.

"Welcome," the queen said, in a low voice.

We scrambled to our feet. "Queen Hana, I—" Feodor spoke up, dusting his hands off on his coat before holding one out to her.

She was younger than I thought she would be – maybe ten years older than me – and much more beautiful. Her eyes twinkled like I imagined the stars did at night.

"You had better sit. We have a good many things to go over today, and I'm sure you're quite exhausted." She swept an elegant arm to a small sofa under a window. I glanced at Feodor, then crossed the room with shaking legs and sat, sinking deep into the plush couch. My breath was ragged, loud in the quiet room.

As we made ourselves comfortable, the queen motioned for the two figures who had brought us here to leave. The sound of their footsteps descending the stairs soon vanished.

The queen stood before us, leaving a few feet of distance, her hands laced together before her chest. Her face was little as I had pictured it: brownish-gold hair tucked tightly back, the coronet framing a rounded and beautiful face. The way her eyebrows arched away made her seem perpetually surprised.

"I hope your journey wasn't too uncomfortable. I know how those two can be. A necessary evil, I'm afraid." She tilted her head sympathetically to the side.

"It was miserable, thank you," I said. I flashed her a grin that felt more like a snarl. "I was convinced we were on our way to the Guild, with all the chanting I heard."

"The Guild!" she exclaimed. "Never. I would *never* send anyone there."

"Why not?" Feodor asked beside me.

The queen began to pace back and forth in front of our sofa. "I've been seeking out information on the goings-on over there – the Guild, I mean – for some time now, but they are a secretive bunch, aren't they? All the eyes and ears I've sent around the city have come back with nothing – or nearly." She stopped pacing and looked at each of us. "It has recently come to my attention that there seems to be a dreyga on the loose in Shard."

A lump caught in my throat. I glanced at Feodor, whose face was expressionless.

"There is," he said evenly.

"And from what I've been able to gather, there's suspicion that you two let him go free."

"Are you sure you don't *live* in the Guild?" I snapped. "You seem to know a good deal about it."

Feodor set a quieting hand gently on my leg.

164

"You needn't hide it," the queen said, resuming her pacing and ignoring my outburst. "So, it's true. My ears around the city have managed to glean me *something*. That's why I brought you here. I thought you might be my best hope."

The world swam a bit, made worse by my occasional glances outside the tower windows to the dizzying city views below. I wasn't certain of anything in that moment, save, perhaps, for my desire to lie flat on the ground.

"The Guild shut me out long ago, so what happens within those magical walls is a mystery. But you two, on the other hand, you freed the Guild's captive dreyga. You went against the Guild, and I don't know why, but it tells me we *might* be on the same side. You might be able to tell me what I need to know."

"What is that?" I asked.

She smiled. "Well, for a start, I'd like to know why my name is all over the city." She descended into another chair and tilted her head, waiting.

Feodor looked at me. I looked at Feodor, then swallowed. "We heard something about you, and I..." I cleared my throat, feeling more like a child than before. "I told the rumour to my father, who is a Magister at the Guild."

"Oh, a rumour," she said delightedly. "Tell me."

"It's said that you might have the final piece of the map," Feodor said plainly, and the room fell silent for a moment.

"The Guild has one they keep framed. Keep safe. And another they hid, likely so no one would know how close they had gotten." He did not, I noticed, mention that it was in his possession. "Now they just need yours, and the map would be complete."

The queen stood once more and crossed to one of the windows, taking in the view in silence. "You heard that I had a piece of the map. Who told you that?"

I slid from the sofa to sit on the floor, my head spinning. We were higher than the tower by the old gates, higher than the topmost floors of the Guild. How ridiculous, to be longing for adventure and trying to save the city, only to be undone by a fear of heights.

"Siya?" Feodor said, his hand resting on my shoulder.

"It's the height," I told him, closing my eyes.

"Oh, forgive me," said the queen. "I like somewhere high up and private for these sorts of talks. Like a bird's nest. You never know who might be lurking on the other side of a wall. Here, there can be nothing but sky." She sat down opposite us again and leaned forward. "Please, tell me. Where did you hear that I possess part of the map?"

"From a woman named Viveka," I told her, leaning my back and shoulders against the sofa. "She found us in the city gardens and asked for the dreyga's freedom in exchange for that rumour."

"Viveka," the queen mused, her eyes travelling once more to the window. "That's a name I haven't heard in a while."

"You know her?" Feodor asked, his hand still on my shoulder.

"Mmm, I do. She once worked for me, here in the palace. A map enchantress, before she got caught up in the world in the city beyond."

There was a long pause while the queen seemed lost in the past.

"Well," the queen said, rising to resume her pacing. "If you were worried that Viveka had done you wrong, you can set your mind at ease. She spoke the truth."

My eyes flicked to her face. Feodor stopped breathing behind me, and the room descended into a deathly silence. Queen Hana nodded. "It's all true," she said softly. "I do have the final piece of the map."

11

"Why, in the name of the gods, if you possessed it did you not return it?" Feodor asked.

The queen met his gaze squarely. "I couldn't do that," she said.

"Then everything they say about you is true!" Feodor cried. He rose to his feet, his face stormy. "That you're heartless and unfeeling, and care nothing about the people of your city. How shameful, to be called a queen!"

"Feodor, sit down," I said, swaying and gripping the wooden arm of the sofa. Outside, the world was tumbling into darkness as night-time made itself a home.

"The rumour of you having the map is spreading around the city. I mentioned it to my father, and before long people I don't know were speaking of it in the streets."

The queen nodded. "Of course they let it spread.

Turning the city against me will only make their efforts easier." She leaned forward. "Tell me something. Do you trust the Guild?"

Silence ticked by. I let my eyes wander to a window, then back again. "No."

"And you, Feodor. Do you trust the Guild?"

He pushed his hair out of his eyes, frustrated. "I don't know." His voice cracked. "But how can *we* trust *you*?"

"Because I'm the only one who can save the city. And I'm the one you want on your side, believe me."

Outside the window, the lights of the city were beginning to twinkle, candles in windows and hearths glowing in a thousand flecks of light. Like the stars hidden from view so long ago, the city was a constellation of lights. I let my eyes trail over to the Guild, and traced the streets that led me home.

"Tell me," the queen said. "Why don't you trust the Guild?"

Obediently, I began listing suspicions. "They had a captive dreyga, to start with," I said. "Why? My father has taken to wearing a necklace I don't remember seeing until recently, although he tries to hide it. Others wear similar necklaces, even Feodor's father, like they're all a part of something we aren't meant to understand. Their vow to protect and respect magic has become something more. An obsession, to the point of delusion. When does something cross between respect and worship? When does magic become a religion, and not a practice?" I blinked, tears stinging my tired eyes.

The queen rose, her features soft and her eyes brimming with compassion. "I think perhaps the Guild crossed that threshold long ago," she said softly. "It's an insidious thing, the abuse of power. But what is important, Siya, is to never stop fighting to bring back the world they've destroyed. To save what you can, and mourn what you can't."

"How do you fight a power like theirs?" I asked, drying my face with the back of my hand. "They are too strong."

"No," the queen said crisply. "Together, we are stronger."

She crossed the room back to the sofa and motioned to it with a graceful sweep of the arm. "I have something to tell you both, and I think it's best if you sit down. I find it comforting to be seated when I learn things that might shake my foundations."

I closed my eyes, dread mingling with exhaustion as I slowly crossed to the sofa. Feodor sat beside me, so close we were touching.

"Now listen closely, and let me finish," the queen said, seating herself across from us and folding her hands. "My words will not be pleasant, but I promise to speak only the truth. It is no more than you deserve." She drew in a long, slow breath. "The Guild is not what you think it is. It teaches magic, it upholds the work of the First Enchanters, who I believe were good and honest, but you are right: it has changed. Their ardour for map magic and all that it can do has blossomed into something dark and wicked. Something that has no place in our world.

"Their task to teach magic and continue its tradition in Sarsova transformed a few decades ago into a need, a yearning to do more. To stretch magic to its limits, to see just how far it can go. It was said that magic built the world, so they began to wonder: could it happen again? Could the world as it is be remapped into something brand new? One built only for magic, with enchanters as leaders and no magicless kings and queens to watch their every move? A world run solely by and for magic?"

Coldness crept from my feet upwards, a slow death that ended in violent shivers.

"And worse still," the queen went on. "Worse than a world run by the Guild, where magic is everything. All the magicless in this world would not survive the remapping. Magicless souls like you and me. Since we don't have magic in our blood to keep us rooted down in the remapping, we would vanish from existence. An incantation spoken into the air, and gone." She made a *poof* motion with her fingers. "Gone for ever. Like death, in a way."

I swallowed, but I felt like I was choking. "But, my father," I whispered, the room blurred. "My father is one of them. He must know what this would do to me."

"Yes, Siya," she told me softly. "Your father surely knows this."

Impossible. My heart splintered like ice. I wanted

nothing more than to be perfectly certain that none of it was true. But I remembered all the ways my father had looked at me differently than my brother and sister over the years. It was not so very hard to believe him capable of it.

"How do you know all this?" Feodor asked quietly.

"I've known for some time," the queen answered. "Through … an enchanter friend of mine. You'll find out soon enough."

Feodor said nothing.

"But they needed more magic than they had," the queen continued. "Can you imagine how much? To create a new world and make another vanish without a trace? More magic than there is in the Guild, in Shard, even, and possibly Sarsova. My spies told me that people have been disappearing. Map enchanters, lowly ones, those without protection."

I slid from the sofa once more, needing to lie flat on the ground. In another moment, I worried my stomach might empty. *My own father.* My own father was a part of this. But if it was true, then *my father* sought to build a world for the magical, and let me vanish into the ether. A world for my brother and sister and mother. For Feodor and Semyon and the Magisters. But not for me. Never for me.

"So, they started finding people with magic who didn't belong to the Guild," I said, thinking of the librarian. "People who could go missing without much fuss."

The queen nodded. "But hunting down those with magic is time-consuming. So, what could they use instead?

What is one thing that seeks magic more than anything else? Feeds on it? Lives for it? Consumes it, again and again and again?"

Her mouth moved, but I stopped hearing the words. A ringing silence pressed against my ears. Around me, the room had changed and fractured, piecing itself together once more into the hall of cells far beneath the Guild. One cell in particular was wreathed in light, everything around it shrouded in darkness. Inside, a coiled and wrathful creature lurked in the shadows, round eyes trained on me.

"Dreygas," Feodor whispered, so low I barely heard it.

"Dreygas," the queen repeated, nodding. "They captured dreygas and brought them to the city. They were using them. Studying them. Learning how they could further the Guild's great ambitions. Teaching them to track down magicians. Keeping them alive by letting them feed on magic. *Feeding* them through their own citizens' magic."

"I saw it," I whispered, pressing my palms into my eyes. "I saw it happen. The librarian. Where were they taking them?"

"I can't say," she said. "But my spies believe they were feeding magical souls to the dreygas, to take their magic. To siphon it into something where it can be stored. To fuel their grand new world. On a larger scale, if we were still a part of Sarsova, they would have dreygas roaming all over the land, siphoning magic and hoarding it for their one goal. No one would be safe. No one magical, anyway."

I sat up, and then lay back down on the floor. I stretched my legs out and closed my eyes. Who cared if there was a queen present? This was all too much.

I imagined what peace felt like. The early morning moments with a book before my brother and sister awoke. The city gardens at twilight, when others were returning home and the trees were empty of souls. The wafting scent of warm bread from a bakery window on my way to the Guild in the morning.

The Guild.

I screwed my eyes shut, as tight as I could.

"But there was only the one," Feodor said, his voice far away, like from a half-waking dream. "A single dreyga could not do a fraction of what they hope to achieve."

"One, that you know of," she said, very seriously. "Why do you think they want the map so badly? Returning Shard to Sarsova would give them access to all the dreygas in the Bleaks, and their plans would know no limits."

I sat up too quickly, my head spinning. "*That's* why the city is cursed," I said, nearly in a shout. "To keep the Guild away from the Bleaks. To keep them away from the dreygas, so that they could never get enough magic. Did *you* help to curse the city?"

"Not me, exactly. I have no magic, don't forget, and I wasn't the queen then." A twinkling smile played at her eyes. "But my mother, Queen Ulyana, she *did* oversee the enchantment when Baba Yaga tried to save Sarsova from the Guild. The palace of Shard has long been the one to possess the enchanted map that keeps the dreygas sequestered in the Bleaks. A different map to the one that cursed the city, but every bit as important. The Guild has been trying to get its hands on it for years now, without drawing too much attention. It's why the palace has been made off limits. No one in or out. It grows a bit lonely, you know." Her eyes wandered to the window, taking in the city that she could see but never touch.

"Baba Yaga," I whispered. Her eyes trailed back to me. "Baba Yaga helped the queen enchant the city to *save* the rest of Sarsova."

The queen nodded. "Yes. She did. As long as the Guild was in Sarsova, and could freely travel to find dreygas, no one was safe. They had to be removed from it altogether. It was easier to send a city wandering than an entire mountain range."

The words rattled around my head, echoing and breaking apart and coming back together again. *Baba Yaga.* The most powerful magician of all.

"Where is she now?" Feodor breathed, standing slowly. "Or is she dead?"

"Gods, no. She's descended directly from the First Enchanters. She has a while to go yet before she passes on. She's here," the queen answered, shifting in her chair. "Somewhere in the city. She's hidden herself behind so many maps I haven't seen her myself in a very long time.

She checks in from time to time. I can find her when I truly need her. She helped me to enchant the palace, to keep the Guild out of it."

"Baba Yaga is in Shard." Feodor paced around the sofa, both palms pressed against his forehead. "I have lost it," he said, shaking his head. "I have lost any understanding I once had of this world."

"It is a lot to take in," Queen Hana said. "I have had far longer to work through it than you have."

"Why didn't you just tell everyone in the city?" I asked. "If the Guild was so terrible, why not make sure everyone knew?"

She sighed and looked at me with heavy eyes. "Do you think I would have been believed? Do you think they would have let me live, if they found it was I who had spread the rumour?"

I said nothing. Feodor shifted uncomfortably.

Some silence gave me a moment to breathe. Then I asked, "What happened to Ulyana, and your father?"

Sadness tore across her face, but only for a moment. "They passed on," she told me. "A few years ago."

"I'm sorry."

She sent me a grateful look, and I wondered how hard it had been for her, locked away in the palace, alone and grieving.

"What now?" I asked, a few moments later. I leaned my head back against the sofa for support.

"Indeed," the queen said, rising and walking to a window. "You mentioned necklaces before. Tell me what you know of them."

"Very little," I answered, as Feodor continued to pace. "I've only caught glimpses, but I believe many in the Guild wear them. The Officials and the Magisters, at least."

"My father wears one," Feodor said. "He never goes anywhere without it."

"I know why," Queen Hana whispered, staring out at the city below. "A hundred years ago, before the city wandered, a crystal called the versha was found in the mountains. It was said to be a gift from the gods to protect those with magic, as dreygas will not go near it. Will not touch it. It repels them in a way we never understood but didn't question, grateful to have some protection from them. A large central stone was often placed in towns around the country to keep the necklaces active. But one by one, as the Guild took over the mining, they began to disappear. The necklaces are pieces of the versha, keeping those in the Guild safe while they study the dreygas. It makes them … untouchable."

Feodor moved to stand beside me where I still lay on the floor, and the room fell silent. Outside, the world had gone dark, easing the turmoil in my stomach now that I couldn't see the blurred sky and trees far below.

"Do you think they have more dreygas?" I asked quietly.

"I'm not sure anyone knows," she answered. "If there

was one, there may be more. It depends on how many they managed to collect before the city was sent wandering."

My breath was ragged.

"The crystal has many uses, though. Perhaps that's where the magic of the missing magicians is going. Perhaps they're storing it. Taking it from the dreygas, somehow. Practising." She shuddered. "The things they are willing to do seems to know no bounds."

"So, just to be clear," Feodor said softly after a moment. "The Guild will eventually find their way into the palace, if they haven't already. They will find the last piece of the map and bring the city back into Sarsova, thus giving them access to all the dreygas in the Bleaks, who they will then use to drain the magic from magical souls to build a new world. And they are safe from those dreygas because they hold the only antidote to their hunger. And there is nothing to be done."

The queen turned back to face us. "You are right, and then wrong. There is always *something* to be done, depending on how hard you believe, and how much you want it. But first, you must find Baba Yaga."

"Oh. How simple," I said weakly. The thought of finding her felt like something from a dream. Everyone knew of her. Everyone knew the story. But the notion of meeting her felt so strange and detached that I couldn't work up any excitement.

The queen smiled. "Perhaps we have talked for long

enough. I know you have had quite a tiring day. I can offer you a place of rest for the night. It is not an hour to be stalking the streets, as you well know. There are far worse things to do that for you."

She drew in a breath, and then crossed the room to the stairs that led out of the tower. No more questions. No more answers. She simply vanished through the door, turning at the last moment to beckon us to follow her.

12

The queen showed us to our rooms herself, weaving us down labyrinthine halls, past winding stairwells and a hundred doors, up to new levels we had not yet seen, and across tiles that were arranged in the pattern and colours of the night sky full of constellations.

"I do not get visitors," she said as she walked, so quickly that I had to jog to keep up. "I'm rather enjoying the company, even if the circumstances leave something to be desired."

She moved with grace and poise, but quickly. Her dress and gold braid danced about as she walked, sweeping across the pristine tiled floors with a soft rushing sound. Now and then, she glanced at us, as though she couldn't quite believe that there were newcomers in her presence. Like she had forgotten what it was like.

And her eyes smiled.

Then she gathered up her skirts into her fists, and carried on even quicker than before.

"Where is everyone?" I asked as we passed empty hall after empty hall.

"Oh, they're around," she said. "But I keep a very small staff these days. You never know who you can trust."

We climbed a wide staircase that led to a hallway full of bedrooms. Each one was comfortably furnished, and a few were lit by warm candelabra. Most seemed to look over the rear gardens of the palace, although everything was shrouded in darkness.

"Choose whichever room you like," the queen said, sweeping an arm up the hallway. "I will see you again in the morning."

And she left us.

I watched her until she disappeared, feeling suddenly lonely in her absence.

Then Feodor and I stood still for a moment, staring at the doors in silence. The past few hours felt like a dream.

"I suppose … we ought to get some rest," Feodor said presently, edging towards one of the doors.

"I suppose so," I said, moving towards the door next to his. My hand rested on the doorframe, but crossing the threshold felt like an end to a day that I still wasn't quite certain had happened. Loneliness began to press in even more, familiar and cold.

"Get some sleep," he told me gently. "Things won't seem so terrible in the morning. They rarely do."

"I think they will," I replied, looking into the room and to the dark windows.

"Then at least you'll be rested enough to face them. Goodnight, Siya."

"Goodnight, Feodor." For a second, I thought about reaching out to stop him. Asking him to stay with me tonight, on a night when the last thing I wanted was to be alone. But I didn't, and he stepped into his room and closed the door. The sound echoed up and down the hallway.

The room was comfortable, even elegant. I stood just inside the door once I'd closed it, taking in the space that was at least half the size of our entire house back home. Four great posts rose up from each corner of the bed, and a gauzy curtain cascaded to the floor on either side. A lit candelabra standing on the floor lit up the room with a flickering, inviting glow, making my shadow dance about. Some unseen servant must have lit it, anticipating our stay. A plush chair sat by the window that looked down into the darkened gardens, and a faded tapestry of a great hall filled with food and instruments and people in colourful dress covered nearly the entirety of one wall. And just inside the door, close to my shoulder, hung a round mirror.

I stared at myself for a long while, longer than I'd ever done before. The girl facing me seemed a stranger, not like anyone I knew. Her dark hair was wild, her cheeks gaunt, her skin pale and eyes reddened.

I turned away, rubbing my fingers along my face like I could erase all the lines and dark circles. Feodor was right. I needed rest, and a good deal of it.

Kicking off my boots, I climbed into the too-large bed from the bottom and crawled beneath the heavy quilt, sinking into the mattress's warm embrace after an arduous, endless day.

And although I had expected to lie there, awake and wondering, thinking, fearing what was to come, sleep plunged into my mind like a nourishing waterfall from a high mountain peak, and I gave myself up to its grasp.

The raven sea of sleep I'd drifted in throughout the night was washed away by the soft *tap tap tapping* at the door. The dull grey wash of morning had barely begun outside the window. I sat up stiffly and allowed my senses to filter back. How deeply I had slept, and how peacefully. All the dark dreams that I had anticipated stayed away, allowing me this one restful, precious night to recover.

The tapping sounded again and I slipped down from the bed and padded across the room to find Feodor standing outside my door.

"I hope I didn't wake you," he said. His hair was rumpled from sleep.

"You did. But come in." I opened the door wider and

tiptoed across the bare floor back to the bed. A small, judgmental voice admonished me for inviting a boy into my room alone, but given that the world as we knew it was tumbling down outside these walls, I didn't care.

I settled back under the quilt. "What brings you here?"

He shifted uneasily. "I woke early and I wanted to talk. But I shouldn't have woken you. I can come back later, if you'd rather."

"You're here now. Stay."

He crossed slowly to the chair and sat, spending a long moment gazing out of the window. Grey light was washing over trees and statues outside, barely visible from my vantage point on the bed. Dew glistened on the tips of leaves, and muffled birdsong found its way in through the closed windows.

I watched him, half hidden under my blanket and sunken into my mattress, remembering the day when our paths had first properly crossed in the Guild's foyer. When Semyon had been rude and Feodor had sent him on his way. It felt like a lifetime ago. We were not the same people we had been, and we might never be them again.

"How do you think it would work?" I asked softly. "The remapping. I don't fully understand it."

He shook his head. "I'm not even certain myself, to be honest. I suppose it would involve sketching out, very carefully, a whole new world in place of this one, and using an unimaginable amount of magic to make it happen. It's … unfathomable."

I didn't reply. After a moment, Feodor spoke up again.

"Our fathers," Feodor whispered. His voice was ragged. "What does this mean about our fathers?"

I rolled over so I could see him better. "It means they are not good people."

"They *must* think they are doing good for someone. Surely. I can't believe that they are so wicked."

"Doing good for a few at the expense of many cannot be called good. I was never very close to my father, and now I know why."

I'd been sad about that once. But not any longer. Now I was angry.

I'm interesting, I had wanted to scream, so many times.

"But you still must love him."

"Yes," I said after thinking it over. "In a way. But if I think that way, I won't be able to do what needs to be done. They must be stopped, Feodor."

"I know. I know. And yet—"

"*And yet?* Remember that you, Feodor, you have magic. You are the special one. There is a place for you in their world. Imagine, for one moment, that there is not."

He swallowed. "I am not defending them," he said. "I could never defend them. I could never imagine a world without you in it. Don't make me try."

My heart thudded as our eyes met. He took a step towards me.

A knock sounded on the door, and we both jumped.

Feodor crossed the room and answered it, to find one of our escorts from yesterday standing outside.

"There is breakfast for you in the dining room," he said. "The queen awaits." Then he dipped his head into a nod, and left us.

"Breakfast with the queen," Feodor said as I climbed down from the bed. "We must be very special guests."

"*I'm* a very special guest," I told him, pulling on my boots. "I don't know about you. But more to the point, neither of us know where the dining room is."

If the palace had been quiet yesterday, it was silent in the morning. No rustling of distant feet. No hint of a door opening or closing nearby. Only our soft footsteps and breaths, and the still, dark palace. A few sconces had been lit here and there, but in between them, the halls fell into shadow that made me move ever so slightly closer to Feodor. The great drapes hung on the windows didn't let in so much as a scrap of light, setting the whole palace to feeling as though it were drenched in midnight.

We wandered back down the staircase we had traversed with the queen, down another hall, down yet another stair, and to the main foyer where we had first entered yesterday. There, our two captors stood guard by the great doors, and pointed a finger to a hallway before I had even opened my mouth to enquire about which way the dining room was.

Only a few doors down the hallway, the dining room

awaited us. An expansive, cavernous room lined with white stone pillars and windows at intervals, with a smooth floor that shimmered in the candlelight and the growing light outside. Here, where the palace faced away from the city, daylight poured in, with no drapes to block it out. A long stone table stood at the very centre, lined with twenty or so chairs that stood perfectly straight, and perfectly positioned. At the far end of the table sat three place settings, and platters and bowls heaped with bread rolls, fresh fruit, spiced porridge with tendrils of steam rising up, a plate with more cheeses than I could count and a large teapot surrounded by three gold teacups.

I placed a hand instinctively on my stomach as it began to rumble, hoping Feodor hadn't heard.

"Oh, good. You found the place." The queen's voice came from behind us. She swept into the room in a soft blue gown that trailed a good distance behind her when she walked but still gave the impression of being nightclothes. She seated herself at the far head of the table, and gestured to the seats on either side of her. "Please. Join me."

I moved faster than Feodor, drawn by hunger, and maybe a little bit of greed.

"You slept well?" the queen said, buttering a roll with more grace than I would ever possess.

"Yes, I did."

She smiled. "I can tell. You look refreshed."

"Ah." I brushed my fingertips along my cheeks, a little

confused, and reached for a vine of berries. Feodor scooped the spiced porridge into a bowl.

"Directly after breakfast, I will give to you the maps to find Baba Yaga. It will not be easy, and it will require some time spent in the city, so I suggest keeping your heads down and avoiding anyone who might recognize you. Your absence from the Guild will be noted by today, I should think."

I popped one of the berries slowly into my mouth, my ravenous appetite diminishing a little. "What if we get caught?" I asked, feeling a bit like the question ought to be asked.

"Oh, don't get caught," she replied with a small laugh. "I doubt even I could save you if they catch you again."

"Will Baba Yaga help us?" Feodor asked, stirring his porridge.

"I think so. She won't want the Guild to succeed any more than I do."

I reached for a few more berries. "But the map is safe here with you," I said. "Isn't it?"

The queen put down her roll and turned to me. A tiny bit of fear came over me. She seemed kind, but there was iron in her face now.

"If you believe that, then I'm afraid you don't know enough about the Guild, Siya. These designs have been in the works for years. Decades. Maybe longer. It is their lifeblood, their sole purpose. They will stop at nothing until the map is theirs. Until the Bleaks are theirs, and all the dreygas within those wretched mountains." She picked up her roll again. "You cannot be a child and pretend if you close your eyes, the problems will vanish."

She was speaking of evil, but these were people I knew: Fredek, Yarik, Ermolai, my father. They had faces and voices and lives.

But even demons can smile and act like angels.

"I spent a good while last night thinking it over," Feodor said, cradling a cup of tea. "Things I had heard that I had brushed aside thinking they were insignificant. Snippets of sentences I'd heard. I wonder why I wasn't included in their plan."

"Your age, I should think," the queen said, pouring tea. "They would want to know you were ready. That you could keep their secret. They would not wish for an uprising."

I imagined the turmoil that would ensue, if everyone knew. I looked at Feodor. A boy, lauded as a strong and capable map enchanter, destined for greatness and a future at the Guild – only for that to be swept away in a matter of days, the facade of power and honour he had looked up to for his whole life shattering.

Breakfast finished quietly. Then the queen rose and beckoned for us to follow her. It was another long walk through the palace, down halls, up stairs, and finally up into another tower like the one where we had met her yesterday. Only, thankfully, with a shorter staircase.

189

The room we emerged in was wide and round, with books lining the walls and a sitting area placed neatly in the centre. A fire already crackled low in the hearth that broke up the shelves, and a wooden box sat on the low table in the middle of the room. A tiny tower library, like a miniature Atheneum, only with more charm and fewer secrets, probably.

"The maps?" I said.

"Of course not," the queen said, pulling a key from where it hung around her neck and sliding it into the lock on the box. Inside lay another key, which she removed delicately, as though it might fall to pieces in her hands. Then she crossed the room to one of the bookshelves, removed a few of the books and exposed a very small door set into the wall of the tower. "I keep that box hidden somewhere far across the palace, and I move it from time to time. It's the best I can do, really, without magic. But sometimes the old ways are the best."

The lock in the small door opened with a small click, and from it, she withdrew a stack of parchments.

Feodor drew a quick breath beside me – his magic, perhaps, recognizing such old and powerful maps. The queen laid them gently on the table and spread them out.

"You will care for these, I am sure," she said, though the tone of her voice dared us not to. "These are our key to help. These are everything."

Feodor brushed his hand over them, gently.

"They are numbered, in order of use. Siya, you should keep them. Just in case."

I swallowed. She meant, in case the dreyga found Feodor.

I tapped a hand gently on his back, unsure if it offered any comfort.

"The first map begins just outside the palace gates. What you must do will vary from time to time, journeying through the city as you know it, stopping for incantations, and opening doors that aren't there. I'm no expert in magic, obviously, but the instructions should be clear. Time is of the essence, but you must not rush through the reading of the maps. One wrong step and you will be lost, or have to start over. Baba Yaga took no chances when she designed these. And you don't want to wind up stuck somewhere that only the Guild could get you out of now, do you?"

Carefully, the queen handed the maps to me, and I took them with steady hands. Sometime over the course of the morning, my fear had abated. Instead I felt ... ready.

A new day was before us.

"Thank you," I said, searching her eyes and finding warmth and certainty there. She believed we could do this, that much was clear.

"And now, so you do not tire too quickly before the journey has even started." She pulled from her pocket another, smaller parchment and gave it to Feodor. He glanced at the drawings and words, then smiled.

"Ah," he said. "I think Siya will appreciate this more than anyone."

"Indeed. And now I must bid you farewell. I will be here, waiting, hoping, and I wish you well on your journey. And though they may not know it yet, the city is counting on you. Everyone is counting on you." She kissed the fingertips of both her hands, then blew them towards us. "Now off you go."

Feodor turned to me and held up the map, beginning the incantation written on the page. I held my breath.

The room around us began to disappear. For a moment we were nowhere, standing in whiteness, nothing above or below or beside us, until shapes began to again materialize, and a second later we were standing just outside the palace wall.

I turned in a full circle.

"No more tower stairs," Feodor said, tucking the map into his coat pocket. "She thought of everything."

"What if someone takes that from you?" I asked, nodding to his pocket.

"It won't do them much good. It only works in one direction."

Just like the maps in the Guild. Sneaky, and useful.

"What now?" Concealed as we were behind the trunk of a very large, old tree, I handed him the map numbered first, moving to block any distant watcher's view. He unfolded it to read.

"Hmm … yes … I see … yes…"

I shifted from one foot to the other, while Feodor studied the map with all the intensity of a Charge worried they might fail a test.

"Is it telling you anything?" I asked finally.

"Oh, yes. Lots of things. Right. We follow this road down into the city and search for Narrow Lane." He folded the map again and tucked it under his coat.

We turned to face the road.

"Are you ready, Siya?" he asked.

"Are *you* ready, Feodor?" I asked.

"I think so." He took a few deep breaths in quick succession. "All right. Let's find Baba Yaga," he said.

We took our first steps back towards the city.

13

Little seemed to have changed in the city – or so we thought at first.

But the longer we walked, the more I noticed that the streets seemed a bit less crowded than usual. People seemed nervous. I could see children's faces pressed against windows, watching longingly as the world went by without them. A number of the familiar peddlers' carts were missing from the bigger streets, though many still remained.

An air of uncertainty hung about, like a fine mist that's easy to ignore until it isn't.

"What do you suppose has everyone hiding indoors?" I whispered, barely moving my mouth as we walked. "Farod? The Guild?"

"Either. Both. Neither," Feodor whispered back, but when I caught a glimpse of his face, worry had run wild in his eyes.

"Illuminating," I said sarcastically. But deep down, I knew the most likely reasons. A dreyga loose in the streets. Bodies drained of magic. People going missing.

Fear lived here now, great and thriving. Fear had crept through doorways and cracked windows like inescapable smoke.

"Quick," Feodor hissed suddenly beside me, and ahead I caught a glimpse of two men walking in our direction, one cloaked in lavender, one in black.

He pulled me quickly towards a shop window. "Oh, fascinating," Feodor said, suddenly bright and chipper, admiring the shop window with books on display. He pointed to a gardener's manual with a gold rose on the cover. "I like … gardening…" I could have laughed if I wasn't frozen by fear.

I stood beside him, keeping my face towards the window no matter how desperately I wanted to look back at the Guild members. Had they seen us? Were they *searching* for us? I imagined a hand reaching out to grab my shoulder, a doorway being drawn up like the one in the library and Feodor and me vanishing through it, never to return.

Sweat dripped into my eyes.

Minutes passed. Maybe years. There was no way to know. But eventually, when no one had come to grab us by the shoulders, Feodor dared a sidelong glance up the street. There was no sign of the Guild members. Only the occasional passer-by, a seller pushing a cart. And finally, I allowed myself to breathe.

"The alley shouldn't be much further," Feodor said under his breath as we continued on down the street, now more watchful than before. Most from the Guild might not recognize us in passing, or from a distance, but if either of our fathers were to be out, or Fredek, or Semyon, any chance of finding Baba Yaga and saving the city – and the world – from the Guild's destruction would be over.

Ahead, a small, old sign with weathered letters read "Narrow Lane". And aptly named it was. The alley was just wide enough to walk down, though Feodor's shoulders – broader than mine – occasionally brushed against the walls on either side.

"I wasn't expecting it to be so narrow," I quipped, to cover the sinking dread at such a close space. But I knew from my years at the Guild that we could not turn around to seek another way. The journey must be made precisely. That was the way with these sorts of maps. Each step along the right course kept the magic of the map working. If we deviated before we had finished the points along the first map, we would be forced to start again.

You could take a zigzag course down the designated road, so long as you didn't leave the road. You could stop on a doorstep, so long as you didn't go in.

"Here," Feodor said softly, pausing to take the parchment out from the safety of his cloak. He read for a moment, then ran a hand along the wall to our right, breathing words so quietly I could barely hear him.

In a moment, a plain wooden door appeared from nowhere, and I pulled the round handle until it slid silently open. We both ducked inside, and Feodor pulled it closed again.

We let a few seconds tick by, listening, waiting.

It was difficult not to imagine I heard footsteps coming towards the door. I placed both hands on my middle, feeling the breath going in and out. Forcing it to slow down.

I wanted to believe that the worst was over. That we were now safe, and somewhere out of sight, but I knew better. It had likely sent us to another point in the city, keeping us moving along its predetermined course. We hadn't vanished, as much as I would like that to be true. We had just been ... relocated.

I half wished I knew less about how map magic worked. How lovely it would be to just follow Feodor along this journey in blissful ignorance of the actual dangers it presented. But alas, working at the Guild had taught me *something*, after all. One wrong step and we would have to go all the way back to the beginning, and time was precious right now. Then there was the possibility of the Guild watching us, waiting to be led directly to Baba Yaga, after all this time. Not to mention any shadow could hide a hungry dreyga, just waiting for a magical meal.

The tunnel seemed empty, and deadly quiet, save for the occasional drop of water splashing somewhere out of sight. With next to no light, other than the faintest hint of a glow far ahead, we were forced to feel along the walls as we made our way forward, working to stay quiet.

And when at last the end of the tunnel came into sight, we found that the glow came from daylight filtering in through the grate at which the tunnel ended. A hole had been cut in the metal, just large enough for a person to pass through if they crawled along on their elbows, like a worm. I glanced at Feodor, wondering if that was meant to be our way forward, and he nodded.

"This will be in no way humiliating," I said in a whisper. Because there was no way to do this gracefully.

Bracing myself with a breath, I moved to crawl forward – then froze. A hiss, or perhaps a low laugh, rattled ever so softly behind us. I spun to face the darkness, but found nothing visible. Only the yawning shadows of the tunnel.

"Go," Feodor said under his breath, pushing me towards the hole in the grate. "Hurry."

I threw myself towards the opening and pulled myself through with my arms. My belly and legs scraped across the damp ground as I hauled myself out the other side, then rolled quickly away to make room for Feodor.

He hauled himself through in seconds, rolling to the side, and ran to lift one of the large stones that littered the mouth of the tunnel on our side of the grate.

"Quick, help me lift it!" he said. Together we heaved and rolled it into the opening of the grate.

Not a second later, a body, running with an inhuman speed, flung itself at the grate. Two hands reached out to clutch the bars. Orange-tinted eyes trained on us.

"Let me through," he said, his voice deeper than I had heard it before.

Feodor didn't move, seemingly rooted to the spot.

The dreyga began to rattle the grate with the kind of strength that made me think he could rip it apart entirely.

"Let me through!" he thundered again, and the words carried on echoing around us, again and again.

"Feodor, hurry," I said, grabbing hold of his hand and pulling him away, stumbling through the tunnel.

The tunnel opened up into a quiet side street by a canal, which explained the dripping sounds. It was a quiet part of the city, with only a few souls milling about, eyeing us curiously.

We rounded a few corners, following the course on the map that Feodor held, and then stopped to catch our breath, leaning against the walls of an old house for support.

"In all the city," I breathed, shaking my head. "In all this space. Farod managed to find us. What wicked luck."

Feodor shook his head. "No, Siya," he said. "No, that wasn't Farod."

I stared at him. "How can there be another one?" I whispered.

Feodor didn't reply.

I shivered, then stood straighter, adjusting my cloak. "Come on," I said. I could worry about where it had come from later. And I *definitely* would.

Feodor glanced at the map once more, then turned, speaking softly to himself, and led me down the empty street.

The buildings were lower here, mostly homes, blacksmith shops and the like. A few pigs were confined to a pen full of mud, and their eyes watched us move past in a way that made me uncomfortable. Everything was unsettling now, and everything seemed to watch us. To know what we were doing, and where we went.

We walked on a winding path, between buildings, across small squares, down quiet streets, until I began to worry that we were lost. That Feodor's fear over being followed by dreygas had clouded his reading of the maps. But finally, we stopped to face an arched doorway that opened on to a narrow staircase. The stairs swept up into darkness, no end in sight.

The edges of the archway shimmered almost imperceptibly, magical and fleeting.

"Up," Feodor said, nodding to the stairway. "Hurry."

I glanced behind instinctively, before darting through the doorway and up the stairs.

The stairs, it turned out, wanted to play a trick on us. Though we were climbing up, my legs felt like we were climbing down. The air grew heavier and darker, like descending into a basement, an earthiness surrounding us. I took to holding on to the wall for support.

When we reached the top – or the bottom – we emerged into an empty, round room. The floor was stone, the walls strips of wood, and there wasn't a single piece of furniture or another door to be seen. I walked in a full circle, my steps growing faster by the moment, then stopped to face Feodor. "Now where?"

Feodor studied the map in the very dim light – light of which I couldn't quite place the source. I always felt like a lamp or a candle was lurking on the edges of my vision, but it vanished when I turned to face it.

While Feodor read the map, I listened. There was the faintest sound coming from *within* the room. *Tap. Tap. Tap.* I spun, searching every inch of the space, but there was nowhere to hide, nowhere a dreyga might be lurking and waiting. No shadowed spaces in which to disappear.

Something brushed my shoulder, bringing with it the very distant sound of footsteps that grew louder, then faded away.

I jumped, stifling a scream. Feodor caught my arm, pulling me into a warm embrace.

"Shh, Siya. This is magic," he said. "The room is empty, but it is occupying space in the city. We might be in someone's home or shop. No one can see us, but the veil between us is only so strong. Their sounds and echoes will linger."

Still trembling, I spun around a few times. The soft

thud thud of steps sounded again, this time by the far wall.

"Can you hear it too?" I asked, on the verge of tears.

"I can. I know it's unsettling, but it helps to know what it is."

"Sorry," I said, swallowing. "I don't have years of magical training behind me. This is all a bit unsettling, and I'm not ashamed to say it."

"You shouldn't be," he said softly.

"Just get me out of here," I demanded, standing straighter. "I don't like it."

The steps were too real, too close. I'd had enough of being followed, and the footsteps only brought that fear back. There was the sadness too. The sadness of feeling so close to the Shard I knew. I reached out, brushing a hand through the air, half wishing an invisible one might grasp mine and pull me to safety. Tug me away from the awfulness that haunted my every footstep.

"I need the second map," he said, folding up the first one and returning it to me. I drew it out and passed it to him, replacing the one he gave me back into my cloak.

Strange, how they just looked like normal maps to me, parchment decked with lines and shapes and road, but followed by incantations written in a language I would never be able to speak. And even if I did, the words would never mean anything. Never do anything.

A moment later, Feodor began a low, rhythmic incantation that filled the room with a pulse. It worked to drown out the footsteps and hollow voices that penetrated our magical veil, and in only seconds, another door appeared on the far side of the room.

I all but ran to it, ready to fling it open and escape, but Feodor grabbed my hand.

"Caution," he breathed by my ear. "The magic is getting stronger. The layers deeper. Things may become less and less certain, and more uneasy, like the people in this room we can't see. Every step must be careful now."

Inside, a wide foyer yawned away from us. Wide staircases split away, winding off to various floors above and below. Down a hallway sat a small room with a sign outside that read *Clerk* – hung at an angle. A door in the wall disappeared behind us as Feodor and I came to a stop and stood perfectly still.

I whirled to face him. "The Guild?" I asked. A thousand thoughts boiled up, none of them good. Was this a trap? Had we been lured here by magic so the Guild could finally capture us? Throw us into the Sanctum far beneath our feet? *Had Feodor done this?*

He studied the map, holding it close to his face to read it in the darkness. "It *is* the Guild," he said after a moment. "It's not labelled, but the floor plan is identical. It's clever, if you think about it."

"How?" I snapped, far too loud. I clapped a hand over my mouth and gritted my teeth. "How is this clever? We shouldn't be here, Feodor. We have to leave."

I made for the grand doors, but Feodor called, "Siya, stop!" so loudly it made me jump. I spun to face him again.

"What? Feodor, if they catch us here, it's over. This will all have been for nothing."

"If you open that door and walk through it, we will have to start this journey over again – or worse. I don't know what sort of magic is tied to these maps, Siya. We might get lost for ever, stuck in the in-between. I might never be able to get us back out. You have to let go of the handle, Siya. You have to." He had moved closer to me while he talked and now he reached out, slowly, and gently lifted my hand from the door. "Please. There are already dreygas following us. If we have to start again, we will never make it. Please don't let this be the end."

I dropped my hand back to my side and turned to face the foyer. "But why the Guild?" I felt oddly nostalgic, like I could make my way over to my desk and set about the day's dull work like nothing had changed.

But this version of the Guild felt dead. Empty.

"Because it's the heart of the magic in the city," Feodor answered. "There's a lot of magic here. It makes working the maps easier, that's for sure. Come on." He reached out to take my hand. "Let's get through here as quickly as we can."

We crossed the foyer with silent steps. It didn't seem like the same building, it was so empty and dark and devoid of life. All the voices of excited Charges and the heavy sighs of their teachers were absent, leaving a deep, echoing void in their wake. Darkness pressed in from everywhere. I couldn't tell if night had fallen in the city, or if this was just how things looked when shrouded by magic, but it made me feel cold. No life. No voices. No movement. Just stone and shadows and silence.

"I don't understand," I said quietly as we climbed a flight of stairs. "If Baba Yaga could spy on the Guild like this, why hasn't she done so already? Why doesn't everyone do it?"

"It's like the room with the footsteps. You may be in the Guild, but you can't see much or hear much. Only bits and pieces, which isn't very useful. Maps like these work with *places*, not people or things. Think of it as space in the city. We are passing through the space that the Guild occupies within Shard, and not so much the actual Guild itself."

"Right," I said, shivering at the memory of those footsteps so close at hand. "When this is over," I said, as we climbed a flight of stairs, "I think I'll have had enough of magic for one non-magical lifetime."

"I can't say I blame you. I wish I could take a break from it all."

I looked at him as we climbed breathlessly. "Why?"

He shrugged. "It's all-consuming. It's all anyone ever talks about. Sometimes I think it would be nice just … to live."

A laugh escaped me. In all my life, I had never once imagined that someone who *did* have magic might not want it.

"It must be hard being so special and magical," I said, trying to keep the bitter note from my voice.

"That's not what I meant," he told me. "Have you ever stopped to think…?" His voice trailed off, and he ran a tired hand over his face. "I know you always wished you were magical, Siya. But don't let that cloud your ability to see what makes *you* special."

I blinked a few times, running over his words again. I couldn't think of what to say, and we had already reached the top of the stairs.

Feodor consulted the map again. "That hallway," he said, pointing and rolling up the map.

I gasped and caught his wrist. "Wait," I whispered.

On the edges of my vision, I saw someone walking towards us, their robes dark and pooling on the floor. Gliding down the hallway towards the stairs where we stood. But when I turned to face them, they disappeared. Gone, without a trace.

A presence brushed past me, one dreadfully familiar, and the faintest hint of my father washed over me. I watched out of the corner of my eye as he made for the stairs – then paused and turned to look back. Turned to look in the direction of us, as though vaguely aware of a presence. Then he shook himself and carried on down the steps, soon vanishing.

Feodor swallowed.

"He didn't see us," he said softly. "No one can see us,

as long as we keep on the right path. Let's carry on. We're almost there."

"I don't like being here." I hugged myself as we walked. "Even on a good day I don't much like being here, but even less so now. It feels like it should be full of ghosts. I hate the emptiness."

"As do I," Feodor agreed, "but the good news is that I think we are almost there. Or getting close."

"How can you tell?" I asked.

"Because I have a map."

"Ah." I slapped my forehead. *Obviously.* Feodor laughed softly as we carried on down the hallway.

"I don't know why I miss the Guild so much," I found myself saying. "Not now that I know what they've been planning. I should hate it – and I do – but I hate seeing it lifeless even more."

"You can miss the good parts of something," Feodor mused. "I know I do. I feel like I grew up here. I had friends here. I wonder what will become of them all. If they would have found themselves so misguided too."

I tried very hard not to feel bad for him, but a small pang of sympathy formed in my heart.

Even though everywhere seemed empty, as if stripped of every artefact that made the Guild the Guild, I stopped now and then to peer into rooms. Rooms I had never been in before. And now and then, out of the corner of my eye, bits of paper or pens or books fluttered for a moment before vanishing. Small glimpses of the Guild as it was, but only for the briefest of moments.

I stopped near the end of the hallway to stare into a room. We couldn't go inside; that would upset the magic. But it was the room I had seen the Magisters in, when they were working to make the globe disappear. *When they had been practising.* This beautiful world in which I lived, gone, and me along with it. Me and all my memories, disappearing for ever.

Part of me wished my father *did* know I was here. So I could tell him how much I knew. He wanted to destroy me, and everyone else like me. So, in turn, why shouldn't I destroy him?

"Siya," Feodor whispered, tugging my arm and leading me through a magical door.

Beyond it, a cavernous stone space. Feodor struck a flint and lit a small candle he had kept tucked away in his pocket – though the light did almost nothing to illuminate the vast room.

"Where is this?" I asked.

"I don't know," he said, holding the candle aloft and turning in circles to take in the space. "But I have a hunch."

I watched his face, the candlelight flickering. It was a perfectly wonderful face, beautiful in every way. And now, illuminated by the golden light he carried, small fires danced in his eyes, excitement and exhaustion and wonder all glowing together.

"I think we're under the city," he said, craning to look up as high as he could. Whatever ceiling was above us stood too high to see, only shadow and nothingness sweeping away.

"How could we be *under* the city?" I asked, keeping close to him for the light. A deep and hungry darkness lurked just beyond the glow of his candle.

"I don't know," he whispered. "But I don't know where else there would be this much space. Magic has rules, but it doesn't always make sense, at least not to me. The city is still in Sarsova, but no one can see it. It's been thrown into a different plane, a different time, maybe. A place with light no one in the world beyond can see. It depends on what sort of magic Baba Yaga used when she drew up the map. But we could be in the layers of stone built beneath Shard, hollowed out by magic only for this journey."

"The more you try to explain it, the less I understand."

I shook my head, reminding myself where we were exactly did not matter as much as reaching our destination. "Where do we go from here?"

Feodor consulted the map. "We have to cross it," he said. "However wide it may be; the map doesn't show scale. Then create a door."

I turned to face the great expanse. Anything could hide in that much darkness. Magisters, dreygas … or something much, much worse. It was the kind of darkness that came only with sleep, the kind where you don't dream but drift on a bed of raven feathers down a river of nothing.

209

"We can't go back," Feodor whispered to me. "No good things wait for us back there."

"Of course not," I told him. "We are obviously going forward."

Neither of us moved.

"This is ridiculous," I announced, and I took the first steps forward into the waiting darkness.

Feodor followed me. The candle worked only to light the ground immediately below and before us, but against the wall of shadow around us, it did nothing. So we clustered together in the small bit of light and made our way forward, one step at a time, half expecting at any moment for something to come clawing its way out of the darkness.

I guessed this was part of the way Baba Yaga kept herself hidden. It didn't only take magic to read the maps and find her; it took strength and will, and a sort of fearlessness.

Time did not exist in the vast emptiness. Every second felt like an hour, and every step seemed to take us nowhere, like running in a dream without moving. How much space lay all around us was impossible to know, but I swept my arms out now and then, terrified when I did so that it might brush against something unseen. Something alive or dead, or *undead*. The dreyga trying to get through the grate snapped back into my mind, and I spun quickly to look behind us.

My fear of the darkness had grown flesh, because I

210

was very nearly certain I saw something beyond the realm of light.

I turned to face forward again, my steps quickening. "I think we should blow out the candle," I whispered, but my voice might as well have been a shout, the way it echoed around us.

"Why?"

"In case anything can see us. We don't know what's down here. We don't know what's following us. Or in front of us. Or above us. Or beneath us, for that matter. Do you see my point? We don't know *anything*."

"It would be hard to tell which way is forward."

"I'm sure you'll figure it out, magical boy," I said.

A second later, Feodor extinguished the candle. The utter darkness melted in around us, filling up every inch of where the light had once fought to keep it at bay. Not a scrap of light showed through to highlight our next step, or make visible a hand held directly before my eyes.

Feodor's hand slowly slipped into mine. I committed how it felt to memory. Squeezing it. Stealing strength from it. Somehow, it was just what I needed, and I smiled in the cover of darkness.

Then onward we walked, our steps slow and careful, feeling out before us all the while. I could feel panic ebb and fall. I wanted to just give in to the fear and scream into the darkness or maybe cry a little bit, just to see if it would make me feel better. But I didn't. Panicking would only lead to missteps and wandering, and we didn't have time for that.

So I breathed, deeply, forcing the air into my lungs slowly, and then back out again.

My hand knocked against something cold and hard. I drew back quickly, my arm trembling, but Feodor wrapped an arm around my shoulders.

"It's the wall," he whispered. "I need only to light the candle for a moment, to read the incantation."

He struck the flint a few times, and the candle burned to life once more. I withdrew, placing my back against the wall so I could stare into the darkness behind us. Shapes kept twitching to life beyond the flickering candlelight, my tired eyes forming beasts where there was nothing. Though I did wish Feodor could work faster. The vulnerability of having the light once more invited dread back into my veins.

Over the low rhythm of his words, I heard something. The distant *tap tap tap tap* of footsteps – *running* footsteps – reached me. Something else was in this chamber. Something that knew we were here.

The wall behind me shifted a bit.

"Hurry," I breathed, hoping my words would not disrupt the incantation. "Something's coming. Hurry."

I could picture the long legs of Farod running towards us at an inhuman speed, hungry and hunting and awful. The tapping grew louder, incessant, drawing closer and closer through the wall of darkness.

"Feodor, hurry," I urged again, every muscle tense. Ready to fly.

Feodor's incantation stopped abruptly, and his hand rattled a metal doorknob.

"Now," he said, flinging open the door. We rushed through it, yanking the handle closed behind us and twisting the lock that appeared only on this side.

Seconds later, something thudded hard against the other side of the door.

A roar of anger and frustration rattled the wood.

"Come," Feodor said, taking my hand. "Trust the lock. It was built for a reason."

As he spoke and we turned away, the lock and bolt rattled as the monster – man – beast – threw himself ceaselessly against it. I wasn't certain it was built to take that kind of force, but Feodor was right. All that we could do now was put as much distance between us and him as possible – and hopefully enough to be more than one step ahead of him.

The door had dropped us in what felt like a ghost town, or at least the empty edges of the city. It was dark, only a dim and filtered light from a few small lanterns here and there, mist rising thick from the ground. The houses seemed empty, soulless windows like the eyes of the dead that had gone dark and lifeless. Perhaps we were still somewhere in the city, or at least a version of the city, changed by the map and magic. We made our way down the street, slowly, eyeing everything as we went. No other souls roamed about, no trace of another person.

At least not at first.

The further we walked, the more I noticed shadows in the corners of my vision, phantom people walking towards us or away from us on the street, then vanishing. I yelped, clasping a hand over my mouth and pointing in the direction I had just seen a man in a cloak. Feodor stared for a long while, then gently pulled my hand from my mouth.

"Remember," he said gently. "As with the Guild. This version of the city and the real one are very close. We bleed into theirs, and they into ours. Think of it as a very thin curtain shielding us. If we stay quiet and keep on the path, they won't know we're here."

I nodded, still shaken.

Maybe I didn't want magic, after all.

"Onwards," Feodor said. "And I think it's time for the final map."

I gave it to him with trembling hands, remembering suddenly the great bed in the palace where I had woken up after such a deep sleep. That's what I wanted again. To sink beneath those blankets and disappear from the world for a while. The world and all her shadows and monsters and fear.

Feodor consulted the new map, directing us down the appropriate streets, glancing behind us now and then to ensure that the door had held the dreyga at bay. Where two buildings were pressed up against each other, he worked a quick incantation that made a narrow alley appear between them. We slipped down it, quickly and quietly, and on the other side, the city seemed to melt away. The buildings were gone, the road empty, with only dead grass and mist as far as the eye could see. An endless field, riddled with darkness. A shadowed, colourless version of the world beyond.

"We carry on here," Feodor said. "Keep on this road. Then the map just … stops."

"What do you mean, *it stops*?"

He turned to show me the parchment, pointing to the road we were on. The markings ceased. No more roads. No more incantations. Just an empty page.

"Is it unfinished?" I asked. Surely we hadn't come all this way, only to find a dead end.

"I don't know," he answered. "We have to find out."

So we walked down the road, the mist swirling and clinging to our legs as we went. Without a single building in sight, the vast openness of the space was unsettling, like the chamber we had just left. As if we had walked off the edges of the last map of the world and there was nothing left to see but darkness and fog. People told stories about lands like this, the devilry of unmapped places where anything could exist. Anything could happen.

And in the space of a heartbeat, we weren't alone any more. Two great figures rose up from the mist, shadows gathering themselves into two tall beasts that drew towards us. Orange eyes gleamed, hands held open and ready. A low hiss escaped from one, bearing all the satisfaction of a dreyga who had finally caught its prey.

I turned to Feodor, fear making me slow. Everything had blurred a bit, lines and smudges surrounding everything. His eyes were heavy, his mouth open, a kind of resigned horror in his face that brought a scream to the base of my throat. That face said everything. *There's nothing we can do.* Magic was no good against something that could destroy it.

They may not kill me for magic, but certainly after they had finished with Feodor, they would rip me apart and scatter my body around, just for the entertainment. Just to make me pay for eluding them for so long.

Perhaps that was why the map ended. Perhaps this was where our journey ended. That was the other thing the stories said. Where the maps ended, death often waited.

They moved closer and closer – one clearly Farod, the other the one we had seen in the tunnel by the grate – stopping only when they stood just before us, side by side. It was difficult to tell them apart at first, save for their different and ill-fitting clothes, as though they had stolen them from previous kills but were too tall or oddly proportioned to ever make them fit right. The laces of their boots were only half done.

"Do we run?" I whispered. "Do we try?"

"I think not," said Feodor. His voice shook, and he cleared his throat. "I don't think we'll get far."

The thought rocked me, death so impossibly close, its vessels looming before us and waiting to deliver us. "I think we're dead anyway," I breathed. The words choked up my throat. I turned my eyes to Farod, letting all the fear and anger and hatred I felt gather in my face until it burned. "Viveka would be ashamed," I whispered to him, because I couldn't find my voice.

"Viveka is as good as dead," Farod said simply, his voice syrupy. "I do not answer to her. I do not answer to anyone."

Silence settled in. A twinge of sorrow pulled at me. Sorrow for Viveka and how certain she had been that Farod cared for her. How misled she had been.

And fear grew larger and larger, filling up my heart. My mind. Knowing that somewhere, Viveka was working to keep Farod in line had offered even a scrap of comfort, until now. She had thought her affection for him could keep him in check. That he wouldn't dare to do anything that might upset her. But she was a fool, it turned out, and dreygas did not like to be restrained.

The Guild would have their hands full trying to control them all, if it ever came to that.

"Viveka loves you, somehow," I said. Perhaps if I pleaded, worked hard enough, I could find the parts of him that were human. Because that's what people said: that dreygas had once been humans, just like us.

217

"I do not love," he said, plainly and coldly. "I do not feel."

"No more talk," said the other dreyga, raising its hands out towards Feodor. They shook a bit with hunger. "No more waiting."

They stepped forward, and neither of us moved. What would we do? Where would we go? Feodor was right: running would be over before it had started. Escape was impossible. And there was nowhere to hide. The map's magic had run out, and even if it hadn't, there wasn't the time to work another incantation. Our journey ended here.

I wondered, briefly, if anyone would ever find our bodies. If anyone else would chance upon this magicked part of the world and find two souls lying here among the mist and darkness. If they would wonder what had brought us here, and why.

The other dreyga grabbed Feodor and flung him to the ground like a rag doll. I screamed, grabbing at Farod's arm as he moved in, as though I were strong enough to stop him, but he shook me off so hard I skittered backwards and landed in a heap on the ground. They had both surrounded Feodor, vying over who got to put a hand directly around his throat, shoving one another roughly away.

Feodor shook his head, over and over, turning to try and see a way out, but always finding a dreyga blocking the way.

"No, no, no," he breathed, again and again.

A flash of light left me blinded. I'd been struggling back to my feet, but stopped and slumped back down again, dazed. As shapes began to filter back in, another form appeared in the mist, a cloaked woman with her hands stretched out before her. I rolled on to my hands and knees, trying to stand but failing.

"Feodor?" I said, my voice cracking. The dreygas had stopped descending on him, hissing and drawing away from the light in the other figure's hand. They shrank back, shrivelling away like scraps of paper consumed by fire.

"You've brought dreygas to my doorstep, whoever you are," said the woman. "Didn't anyone teach you better than that?"

Ah. I knew that voice, even though we'd never met.

A certainty settled into my shaking bones as she made her way closer: we had found Baba Yaga. Or she had found us.

A low, hungry growl rose up from Farod as Baba Yaga came closer.

She had parchment in her hands and she spoke in a low and measured tone, words too far away to hear. But she wasn't fast enough for the dreyga; in a blur of movement, the two dreygas launched towards her in tandem, sending the three figures tumbling into the dusty road.

Feodor raised himself up. I crawled over to him on my hands and knees, cradling his head as the scuffle grew louder. Then, in a flash of movement so jarring I had to blink to be sure it was real, both dreygas were drawn through the air by a violent rush of wind and *into* the trunks of two trees that rose up from the ground with a great, thundering groan. The bark and knots swallowed them, their bodies vanishing inside.

A grim quiet came over us, over this strange, dark world in which we had found ourselves. Fog lapped around us. Our breathing was the only thing to break the silence, deep, shuddering breaths born of exhaustion and fear. Their faces were still only just visible through large, knotted holes in the trees, orange eyes gleaming with malice and threats.

Baba Yaga rose and dusted herself off. A thick black cloak hung from her shoulders, and every movement was sharp and deliberate. Her eyes only barely glanced at us as she brushed a few tendrils of dark hair from her face. "Very well," she said, as though the entire ordeal had been wildly inconvenient. "Follow me, then." And she turned without so much as sending us a second glance and made off down the road.

14

The empty, misty openness was broken only by the road, and the silence only by our soft footsteps as we followed Baba Yaga. I watched Feodor often, frightened by his silence after brushing so closely with death. How scared had he been?

Tears ran silently down my face. Feodor had so nearly died. *I had so nearly lost him.*

"I'm fine, Siya," Feodor said suddenly. He was smiling. "I can feel you worrying."

"You could be dead," I said.

"But I am not dead," he said firmly. "I am not dead." His voice was gentle.

"You will be if you do not hurry up," called Baba Yaga from ahead of us.

The sudden interruption made us both jump, then

hurry to close the distance between us. We had come upon a small, dark wood that sat to the right of the road. The trees were thorny and black, the twisted branches intermingled to form knots. Deep in the strange trees, a crooked cottage sat menacingly, the thatched roof resting at a precarious angle and two uneven windows staring back like eyes.

Around the house was a fence of bones that clicked and clattered and drew back as Baba Yaga ascended the path towards the house. A candle shone from a skull hanging on a lantern post, shedding yellow light on the odd dwelling.

"In you go," she called, without turning around. "Don't mind the bones. They think they're my watchdogs sometimes." And she disappeared into the house.

Feodor and I paused for a long moment, staring silently at the cottage. Of all the ways in which I had imagined us encountering Baba Yaga, this had not been one of them.

A battle with dreygas, a cottage deep in a wicked wood surrounded by living bones.

Nothing in the Atheneum had quite prepared me for this.

I took the first halting step forward, leaving the road to enter the path lined in bones. They began to shudder as I approached, leaping and lashing out as if to nip at my feet as I went by. I refused to look at them, keeping my chin defiantly high and my eyes fixed only on the house. Even the house seemed to wish us away, though, the eye windows narrowing and glaring, the balusters of the small porch like gritted teeth, snarling.

Baba Yaga had left the door ajar and we stepped inside.

A great stone hearth took up most of one wall, a large black pot simmering over the fire. Dried fruit and herbs and flowers hung in bunches all around the walls, the air thick with the scent of it all. A rough-hewn wooden table sat near to the hearth, covered with parchments, a few mismatched bowls, some wooden spoons and a handful of books. Baskets of various vegetables and loaves of bread lined a wall, some even stacked atop each other. A birdcage with the bones of some winged creature hung from the ceiling, close to my head.

Through a small, arched door, I saw what looked like a bed.

I supposed, if you could make any house you wished with map magic, there were stranger or worse houses to make. I couldn't think of what those might be, at present, but I'm sure they were out there.

"Have a seat, won't you? It frays the nerves when people loom so." The magician nudged two crooked wooden stools towards us and we sat, slowly. "Well, get to it. What brings you here? It's been years since the queen has sent anyone to find me. Has chaos come to the city at last?" She set about stirring her pot and dropping in bits of dried herbs as she spoke, rarely throwing us a glance.

"Chaos, and all its brothers and sisters," I said tiredly.

She shot me a narrow look that said she was in no mood for guessing games.

I cleared my throat. "Let me see… The Guild is on the brink of remapping the world into something brand new, entirely for the magical, where they will have no one to answer to. The magicless of the world, such as myself" – I placed a hand on my chest – "will not survive the remapping. They have at least two dreygas in their possession that we think they might be using to drain people of their magic. They had two pieces of the map and now know that Queen Hana has the third" – *thanks to me*, I thought bitterly – "and they've taken to wearing crystal necklaces that they never seem to go without. So, now we have come to you to ask for help." I drummed my fingers nervously on the table, watching as she stared at me with wide eyes.

Then her eyes darted up towards the ceiling, and she sighed. "Give me strength."

I glanced at Feodor, who waited patiently, watching Baba Yaga curiously.

"Yes," she snapped. "I noticed the dreygas. I always suspected they had held on to some, though they'll need many more if they're going to see this through."

"How did they get them? Capture them, I mean? There are no dreygas in the city. Nowhere to find them."

"They captured them *before* the curse," Baba Yaga said. "Before the city began to wander. It was I who discovered it. I was off travelling through Sarsova to find some rare parchments, cutting through the Bleaks on my return to Shard to save some time, but taking precautions, of course. You needn't look at me like that," she said, noticing Feodor's shocked expression. "I knew I was the only one powerful enough to survive a trip near where the dreygas were banished. So imagine my surprise when I came to a small wood near the base of the mountains to find members of the Guild hauling cages of dreygas on to carts. I thought I must have been dreaming at first. *The Guild* in the Bleaks? Captive dreygas? Who had ever heard of such a thing?" She threw her palms up in bewilderment. "I tried to stop them, of course. I had begun to hear rumours of the world they wanted, of one without useless humans without magic. Those rumours had started long before, and I'd kept my ear to the ground for them, but as far as I could tell, they had remained only rumours. Until then. I waited, and I watched. I kept out of sight for a few days, and those mountains are bloody cold, mind you. But I stayed there all the same, listening to their nonsense about gathering as many dreygas as they could for some insidious plan involving dreygas and a new, magical world. I think I knew then what I had to do. Banishing the city, and all that. Before they got their hands on any more." She shook her head in a way that said it was all too much.

She stirred the pot and then clanged the spoon loudly on the edge to clear off the remnants of what looked like some sort of cabbage stew, her anger speaking through every movement.

"I returned to the city and tried to gather what support I could against the Guild, but there was little reason for anyone to believe me, and before long, the Guild tried hard to silence me. Sneaking dreygas into my home to murder me, even sending Guild members with swords. Anything to do the job so that their secret would die with me. But I stayed one step ahead of them and did the only thing I could think to do to cut the Guild off from the Bleaks and their steady supply of dreygas."

"The curse," Feodor breathed.

"The curse," Baba Yaga replied. "I thought if the city was taken away from Sarsova, then they couldn't reach the mountains. They couldn't reach the dreygas, and their plan would be ruined. There was little I could do about the dreygas already in their possession, but I knew it wouldn't be enough to achieve their goal. I simply had to keep them from ever getting more."

"How did you do it?" Feodor asked. "Move a whole city? And keep moving it?" Fascination tinged his voice.

"Magic is like a muscle," Baba Yaga answered simply. "It gets stronger the more you use it. Binding the city to the map in the first place was difficult and exhausting, but it has gotten easier as time has worn on. It also doesn't hurt to be related to one of the First Enchanters." She tasted whatever was in the pot. "I upkeep it every day, sending it to a new destination, off on some new journey to which there will never be an end. Poor thing."

"Can people see it?" I asked. "People in Sarsova?"

"No. Of course they can't. Imagine! A great, creaking city trundling by. I can think of no greater nightmare fuel than that. No, no one can see it. An impression of it, perhaps. A bit of swirling snow left in its wake, but nothing more."

I tried to imagine how that would look, feel, to someone on the outside. Someone standing amidst the snow in Sarsova, catching a wisp of something brushing past. Seeing the snow ever so slightly disturbed, the air then going still.

She pulled up a stool and sat down across from us, grabbing some sewing off the table to keep her fingers busy. "So, you mentioned necklaces."

"Yes," I said. "Both of our fathers wear them, but they didn't always. They're crystals."

"They still work," she said softly, her eyes on her work. "That's interesting. I'd hoped the crystals would have no potency, with the city wandering."

"The necklaces seem to protect them from their own dreygas," Feodor said. "It's how they can go near them without getting killed. Some of them, anyway. The ones who *matter*, like the Magisters."

"It can do a good deal more than ward off dreygas. It can hold on to magic like the dreygas can. Store it, for future use. One way or another, I'm certain that they're using it for more than just protection." She shook her head. "It sounds to me like perhaps they found more of the map recently, and as they get closer to freeing the city, they are training for their ultimate goal more, in earnest. Capturing magical souls from the city to practise feeding them to the dreygas, and storing the magic. Letting the dreygas keep some of it for themselves. Well," Baba Yaga said, matter-of-factly, "I can only hope that you're here because you've come to the same conclusion as me, and you want my help in doing it."

We both waited, expectantly. I drummed my fingers on the table again, until she cut her eyes at me, and I stopped.

Then she spoke. "The Guild has to be destroyed, if you're ever going to save the city."

Something in her words slipped into my soul as though it was made for me. She was right, and I knew it, and somewhere deep inside, I had always known it. If all of this was true, then the world would never be safe while the Guild still remained. They would always recover. Always find new ways to begin the work again.

But Feodor's face was clouded.

"You have the advantage of being able to slip in and out of the Guild, without being noticed. I don't. They'll sense my magic a mile away."

"It's just that…" Feodor started, and then trailed off. "Does destroying the Guild make us any better than them?"

I opened my mouth to answer, but Baba Yaga beat me

to it.

"Yes," she said flatly. "Destroy the Guild, and you'll be saving both the magical and magicless. Let them carry on, and you will save only the magical. Feel free to correct me, but I think you'll find the numbers make sense." There was a bite to her words.

"Feodor," I said, very slowly. He looked over at me, torment in his eyes. "You know that I have no love for the Guild. But this isn't about that." *Not much, at least*, I thought. "This is about the people. Think about all the people across Sarsova, and in Shard alone, who don't know that their life hangs in the balance. People just like me."

He swallowed, but did not break my gaze. "You won't just be saving their lives," I told him gently. "You'll be saving mine too." I hoped, as I said the words, that his lifetime of being fed words about how magic was the only thing that mattered had at least begun to crack a little.

His jaw tightened with strength.

"What do we have to do?" he asked Baba Yaga.

She gave one brief, satisfied nod. "I'm afraid if you are to have any luck in stopping the Guild, you are going to have to take away their crystal. The mother crystal, not the necklaces. As long as they have it, you are as good as useless against them. The necklaces are an extension of the larger crystal, giving them more range to roam about. But if they stray too far, or the crystal is taken away, they will do nothing to protect them."

"How will that help us?" I asked, a bit sceptically.

"So you can use the dreygas against them," she said, as though that was perfectly obvious.

"Wait," Feodor started. "You cannot mean for us to remove the mother crystal from the Guild itself. From the Requiem, where no one is allowed to go. It is a sacred place to the Guild, where they bury their Elders. That would be impossible."

"More impossible than finding me? Than freeing the dreyga? Than an entire city wandering about? I think perhaps you ought to change your definition of *impossible*, young enchanter, or drop the word entirely."

"How do you know about the dreyga?"

"I know a good many things, I'm afraid. Removing myself from the city does not mean I don't know what goes on. I send eyes in my stead, winged things to collect messages from the palace. A bird or a bat can always travel without suspicion."

My eyes travelled to the bones in the birdcage, and Baba Yaga followed my gaze.

"It was old age, if you're wondering."

"That's comforting." But it wasn't. Not really.

Feodor shook his head. "But how?"

Baba Yaga set her sewing down. "You haven't heard my plan yet, and it's a very good one, and it could mean ridding the world of these deadly designs they've spent so many

230

years cooking up, and a good deal more. Saving the city. Returning to Sarsova. All the things I suspect you want, but also think are *impossible*."

Feodor leaned back in his chair. I could tell that his knowledge of the Guild and the difficulties her suggestion posed were warring with his desire to see it through. "It cannot be done," he said, shaking his head.

"It cannot be done!" Baba Yaga repeated. "They're my favourite words, you know."

"They have more people," Feodor said helplessly. "More strength. More magic. More of everything."

"But we have two dreygas, in case you've forgotten."

I sat up very straight, my eyes darting nervously towards the door. "I thought they were dead," I said. I had hoped they were dead, more like.

Baba Yaga scoffed. "Please. You don't destroy a weapon when you're headed for a war, Siya. That would be silly."

"I don't know how it found us," I said helplessly. "It seemed to be ... tracking us, somehow."

"Of course it was tracking you. Or rather, *him*." Baba Yaga nodded towards Feodor. "Intentionally, no doubt."

"The Guild released a dreyga to hunt down and kill Feodor? He's the next Elder's son." Even saying it out loud tasted sour.

Baba Yaga let out a little laugh. "You give them far too much credit, girl," she said. "These are the very same people who seek to ruin and rebuild the world. One boy's soul is a drop in the ocean. They'll sacrifice whoever they need to, if it means bringing them closer to their goal."

Feodor stared at her, his eyes so full of pain that I could hardly bear to look. "But that's..."

"Please," I said, making a weak joke. "I can't hear the word impossible again, or I might cry." His eyes narrowed, but he stayed silent. "All right," I said, placing both hands on the table. "Assuming we can steal the crystal from the Guild, and that's a big assumption, and assuming we don't get caught, which, again, is a big assumption, what then? What is this plan of yours?"

Baba Yaga cracked a wry, dangerous smile. "Finally," she said. "I'm glad you asked."

15

We slept on the enchanter's floor that night, on rough blankets with the snarling bones lurking just outside. It felt like being in a dream, so different was it from the everyday life we had led back in the city. I stared at the dark ceiling for what felt like hours, going over her plan again and again. Wondering if I was strong enough. Wondering where the line was between what was right and what was wrong.

The journey back to the city was easier than the journey to find Baba Yaga. She sent us with a map that dropped us off near the tower we had climbed together, away from prying eyes who might notice us.

When Feodor and I went our separate ways, coldness sank in with the loneliness.

Being back in the city, no longer separated by that

gossamer thread, was jarring. I wasn't the same person who used to live here, and it wasn't the same city I used to call home. The buildings were the same, the cobblestones hadn't changed, and the smells that clung to the air were the same as they had always been. But at its heart, Shard had changed. The way I looked at it would never be the same again.

I jumped at every noise, saw the face of a dreyga in everyone I passed.

The city had changed. My city.

Fear lingered in every face, a grim silence falling between people who might once have held conversation. Heaviness filled the air, unrelenting and unwelcome. The shadows seemed darker, noises louder, the sense of being seen or watched almost unbearable. I shrank into my hood, hiding from the city as I passed down the street, carrying a tray of baked goods. Everyone was frightened. The escaped dreygas, which must have been spotted by now, the missing magical souls, like the librarian… The city knew now. You could feel it sitting thick in the air.

Familiar, comforting scents of apple and honey wafted over to me, but they made my stomach clench. Nerves made the world a blur.

My feet drew to a stop when the great, menacing form of the Guild rose up before me. It too had changed for ever. The familiar doors were no longer familiar. The grand, rounded walls that had been as a second home to me now felt like a dungeon cell, harbouring secrets and power-hungry murderers. My years spent longing for change hadn't prepared me for this.

A few Guild members came and went through the large doors, their heads down and robes sweeping the ground.

I cleared my throat. I stretched my neck until a soft crack sounded.

Then I held the tray of baked goods higher, and marched towards the doors.

The foyer was largely empty, so I crossed to another Clerk's office and tapped on the door. A woman I only knew in passing, Yeva, popped her head out a moment later, and her face clouded over.

"Siya," she breathed, looking past me and around the foyer. "I don't believe you are meant to be here."

"I know. I just brought something for my father, from Mama. Have you seen him about?"

She shook her head, her eyes wide and worried. "No, but I heard he was looking for you."

"Perhaps you might fetch him for me?" I asked. Her eyes darted down to the tray of pastries, and she bit her lip, uncertain. "Very well. Wait here." And she hurried off.

I eased back to lean against the wall and wait, tension growing within me. I had been the one urging action against the Guild, but now that I was here, it seemed, as Feodor had said, *impossible*. This was the right thing, wasn't it? I had asked myself the same question over and over again since yesterday.

It was all so much. For a moment, I doubted whether I had what it took to see this through. My legs began to shake beneath me, and I shifted to try to make them stop.

Then, from the top of the stairs, a group of Magisters appeared. My father emerged from the group and descended the stairs, slowly, keeping his eyes ever on me. His smoothed-back hair was tied in a knot behind his head. I used to wonder as a child if he liked it long, or was simply too busy at the Guild to bother cutting it.

I closed some of the space between us and met him at the bottom of the stairs.

"Good morning, Father," I said, a cheerful greeting. "These are for you. A gift from Mama. She would have brought them, but I wanted a bit of fresh air."

"You haven't been at home," he breathed, eyes never leaving my face.

"I was away for a bit. Seeing a friend, you know—"

"Anastasiya." His voice silenced me, rattling the floor.

The faintest spark of anger glowed to life within me. How dare he speak to me like that when I knew what he had done? What he still wanted to do. His brown-flecked green eyes bored into mine. "Where have you been, Siya?" he asked.

"I can tell you," I said, my eyes meeting his, "when we're alone."

A shadow passed over his face, only briefly, but he took the tray of pastries and turned away.

"See to it that she doesn't leave," he said to Semyon, who was lurking nearby.

My father turned to walk up the stairs, flanked by the other Magisters. Semyon glared at me and I glared back. "He's been looking for you," Semyon hissed. "Everyone has been looking for you."

"Why am I in such demand?"

"Perhaps they're worried you might do something more foolish than release a dreyga," he whispered. He glanced around, to be sure no one else had heard him.

"Well, I'm here now," I said. My gaze darted between my father walking up the stairs and the great doors of the Guild. "I didn't think someone as important as you would enjoy being a childminder."

He smiled, though it looked more like a snarl, and took a step towards me. And then behind me, I heard the great doors of the Guild creak open.

I spun round. Farod prowled in, followed closely by the other dreyga, newly released from Baba Yaga's magic.

A dead silence passed through the grand foyer, and we all froze, even the Magisters partway up the stairs. Everyone stared, perhaps wondering if their eyes deceived them. Beside me, Semyon had gone very pale. His stunned silence was a delicious gift.

How do you like that? I wanted to ask the Magisters. I

watched Semyon's face for a moment, fighting off the urge to say, *What's more foolish than freeing a dreyga? Releasing it back into the Guild.*

Farod and his companion took their time making an entrance, striding to the middle of the foyer and looking around, drinking it in, taking stock of all the magic to be had in such a confined space.

They looked more man than monster here. They had faces and arms and legs, and wore clothes, if a little tattered. But inside, a ceaseless hunger burned that controlled their every move. Their every second. And that hunger burned hot and fierce now.

Someone, somewhere in the foyer, screamed. The screams caught fire as Farod drew in a long, readying breath. A second later, people began to run in all directions. Wildly. Anywhere they could. Through doors, across the foyer, up or down the stairs. Anywhere that might put more distance between them and the dreygas.

Chaos.

Farod broke into a run, crossing the hall in seconds. Baba Yaga had shown the dreygas magical drawings of those responsible for their imprisonment and torture. They knew who to hunt.

I noticed Semyon slinking away into the shadows, terrified into silence. I backed down a hallway and then broke into a run.

I began to recite the directions I had been given by Baba

238

Yaga out loud, drowning out the noise behind me. *"Down the hall to the blue door. Take those stairs down. Follow that hallway to the right."* My breath caught in my chest. I passed a few curious souls, wondering at all the noise. *"Take the three steps down, and then the spiral stairwell will lead you down."*

Much like the stairwell that led into the Sanctum, this one wound around and around, dizzyingly steep and narrow. My feet slipped several times, and I was forced to cling to the centre pole to keep from tumbling the rest of the way down.

"Why does this city have so many damned stairs in the first place?" I groaned aloud, because it made me feel less alone.

When at last I reached the bottom, leaping the last few steps and thudding to the floor, I nearly crashed into Feodor's waiting form.

He wrapped me in a hug, and for a brief moment I clung to him.

"Did he come?" Feodor whispered into my hair. "Did Farod come?"

"He did," I said through a sob. "They both came."

Baba Yaga had lured them to our aid with the promise of all the magic they could ever want, waiting to be consumed. It hadn't been easy, because trying to reason with dreygas was not something any of us had practice doing, but they had agreed.

The gods only knew at what price.

"We have to go," Feodor said, and he gently took my hand to pull me along the tunnel.

As with the tunnel through the dungeon, this part of the Guild had all the markings of an ancient place. Old stone, writing on the walls too faded to read, iron candelabra standing here and there on the floor. There was more than one route to the Requiem, but we had chosen the one that was the most direct from the foyer. Time was precious.

A few darkened doorways branched off from the hall, leading to older and stranger places, I suspected, but we carried on and on. At last the end of the long tunnel loomed ahead. In the centre of the wall at the end was an arched door with a large, round handle. It groaned when Feodor lifted it, from age and disuse.

The door creaked open with a great, sleepy whine. Inside lay darkness. I took one of the candles from the closest iron sconce and was about to pass through the door when I stopped, something above it catching my eye.

I held the candle high.

"The way to the dead is silent."

I drew back a step. "It's an old burial saying," Feodor told me. "Don't let it frighten you. They are asking for respectful silence beyond this door." He nodded to the opening. "Come," he said. "We mustn't keep the dead waiting."

"Yes, we can," I said back, keeping an eye on the words as we passed under the arch. They chilled every bone in my body.

Inside was a wide, low tunnel that banked sharply down and wound in slow curves, taking us further and further into the ground. Faces carved in stone lined the walls, their unseeing eyes watching our every step. I held the gazes of some as we passed by, old Elders who had been dead since Sarsova was still young. My eyes narrowed, glowering at these men who had laid the foundations of today's Guild. Begun the work that had led to so much destruction.

Maybe they didn't know what would happen in our time, and how far the guild would try to bend and break the limits of magic that had been laid out so early on. But there was no one else to blame.

"Stop," Feodor hissed, shrinking against the wall. I followed him in the space of a heartbeat, holding my breath. He pointed slowly towards the end of the tunnel in the direction we were walking, where another great door like the one we had just passed through waited, closed.

Standing before it were two Guild guards. And unlike the apparition in the Sanctum, these guards were very real. Their gold cloaks reached the floor, a spear in each hand, standing on either side of the door and facing the hall. Hoods shielded most of their face, but the occasional movement of breathing or shifting gave away how human they were. No magical spectres here.

241

I extinguished the candle as hot wax dripped on to my hand. My eyes roamed the rock outcroppings that formed almost pillars at intervals along the walls, becoming archways that ran around the ceiling.

The hint of a shoulder was just barely visible, across the hall and down.

"She's here," I whispered. I had forgotten what relief felt like. "She's here."

"Are you ready?" Feodor asked, glancing at me in the dim light.

"Do I have the option to say no?"

He looked back at the guards. "Um…"

"I'm ready," I told him.

He sighed, readying himself, then let out a low, quick whistle. The guards jolted at the sound, but Viveka was upon them before they knew she was there. Her knife was in one hand, a mace in the other, and she moved with the speed and grace of someone who had either killed before, or spent a good deal of time surviving.

She had been eager to help us, with the promise of us working with Baba Yaga to eventually free the city, and to let her and Farod roam free in the mountains for ever. She would keep searching for the love she was certain Farod felt for her, deep down.

With their attention occupied, Feodor and I crept along the wall, keeping our movements slow and out of sight. When we had reached the end of the hallway, with the fight still raging close by, I slipped forward and pulled on the round door handle until it opened just wide enough for us to sneak inside, then pulled it closed behind us.

The damp Requiem embraced us.

There was one lantern lit in the room, one I had heard was never allowed to go out. An eternal flame burning for the lives buried here. Though the former Elders weren't so much buried as resting in large, rectangular tombs with sharp corners and engraved plaques bearing their names and legacies. They rested on a floor made of smooth stones, time-worn from previous visitors coming to pay their respects. Only Magisters and the Elder were ever allowed down here, though. The occasional Official, if they had a very good reason. Never Charges. Never, *ever* a Clerk.

The ceiling was domed, though the room was rectangular, and unlit iron candelabra stood at regular intervals throughout the room. Who would need to light so many candles in a tomb I couldn't imagine, unless they played a part in some secret ritual. Faded paintings lined the walls in places, chipped away or seared by a candle standing too close, but pieces of them remained. A large globe being painted with a map by a celestial being, clearly a god. The shape of the Guild, the great building above us, held aloft in a sky painted with the glow of heaven, the shadowed world below it. Venerated. Worshipped.

The clanging and shouting outside the room was a

reminder not to linger. I moved forward, passing between the rows of tombs as dust swirled about my feet.

Awe filled Feodor's eyes as we made our way along.

Then, beyond an old statue of a woman bending down to pay her respects to one of the many tombs, we found it.

The crystal rested atop an ornate plinth, the subtle shimmer from candlelight acting in stark contrast to the general sense of death that haunted the room. It wasn't quite hidden, but one might not notice it when they first entered the room. The statues and other tombs blocked it from sight. It was perhaps twice the size of my head, a sort of brownish-golden colour in the dim light, with places where it had been chipped away to form the necklaces worn by the Guild members. A crystalline sound tinted the air around it, like small reverberations that could only barely be heard. A song, in a way.

Feodor came to stand beside me.

"It's not what I expected," he said.

"What were you expecting?"

He shrugged, still staring. "I don't know. Something bigger."

I pulled open the shoulder bag I had kept tucked up under my cloak and, with Feodor's help, heaved the crystal into it. It was heavier than it looked, and I doubled over with the sudden weight. At that moment, the Guards charged in.

"Feodor!" I screamed. The parchment Baba Yaga had given us as a way out was already in his hand. He gripped it steadily, his lips moving, as we backed away towards the far wall. My arms were aching with the weight of the crystal.

"Stop," one of the guards shouted. Through the cracked doorway behind them, I saw an injured Viveka roll over, but she didn't stand. "Stop, now." Their spears were pointed at us, gleaming despite the dim light.

Our backs thudded against the wall, with nowhere left to go.

"Hurry," I breathed, clutching the bag close to my chest. "Please, hurry."

The guards were getting closer, their spears lifted, the dull light glinting off the blade... Losing the crystal meant losing our last chance to stop the Guild. With it, they could do everything. Finish everything they had set out to do. Thousands of dreygas in the Bleaks would become theirs, spelling the end for me, and everyone like me.

"Put it back," the guard repeated, close enough now that their spears nearly touched our faces.

"Feodor..." I said through my teeth, trembling at the weight of the crystal. "Not to rush you or anything, but—"

"Now," he said quickly, whirling and yanking open a door handle. I dashed through, Feodor followed – but he was yanked back. A guard held a blade to his throat.

"Hand it over," the guard said to me. "Now."

I hesitated. Feodor gave me the smallest shake of the head. And then in an instant, the guard was knocked from his feet, the other slumped beside him. Viveka, injured but upright, stood panting behind them.

"Go," she hissed, before crumpling to the floor.

Feodor rushed through the door and pulled it closed behind him.

16

The door had led us to a far part of the city, a quiet alleyway with no other souls about. We stopped to catch our breath. I could feel tears rising. There were two dreygas loose in the Guild. *We had done that.* No one in the Guild was safe now, with the crystal so far away, the necklaces rendered useless. *We had done that.* Viveka was either dead or dying. *We had done that.*

"We are alive," Feodor told me, holding both of my shoulders to look into my eyes. "We are alive, and they might not know it, but the city is counting on us to save them. Sarsova is counting on us. We are alive, and we can still save them. You understand? That is what matters."

I nodded, though his words felt vague and far away, the images of everything that had happened branded into my vision.

247

"Here, let me help you." He took the bag with the crystal from my shoulders and strapped it over his own, tucking it away under his coat. "Stay focused on the present, Siya," he said gently. "Stay focused on the task at hand. We find the queen. That's all. That's the next step."

I nodded. He was right. Just one more step.

We kept to the side streets as we made our way towards the palace. Word of what had happened in the Guild seemed to have reached the city. It was the only subject on anyone's lips, *dreyga* ringing out and permeating the air. I hummed to drown it out.

Feodor led us back to the tree just beyond the wall, where we had come out after walking through the door in the tower. One of the queen's guards was watching and waiting to let us in.

The silence of the palace closed in, and I stopped to drink it up. To soak in the peace and quiet that stood in stark contrast to the day. The screams died away. The clanging of weapons vanished. The shouting of the Requiem guards faded. The gentle hum of thoughts and distant drumming of my heartbeat were the only sounds known to me once more, and the calm very nearly brought on tears.

I shrank against the wall, sliding my back down until I sat on the floor. Feodor turned, standing over me, studying my face with a heavy expression.

Down the hall, our escort paused to wait for us, then

said, "Her Majesty will see you in the dining room, as soon as may be."

"Thank you," Feodor told him. "We won't be a moment."

When we were alone in the hall, he knelt to face me.

"You were very brave, Siya," he said quietly.

A tear rolled down my cheek to my lips. "I'm not a child," I whispered. "You don't have to treat me like one. It was just … I knew it would be terrible. But the screams and the running. How many are dead now, Feodor? How many people did we kill?"

"Siya," he said, then let his voice trail off. In place of words, he placed a kiss on my forehead and let it linger. Warmth and comfort and a feeling of home overwhelming me. When he pulled away, he kept his face close to mine, a hand under my chin that wiped away a tear.

"I want to kiss you properly," he said, a flush tinging his cheeks. "If that's all right with you. One day, I mean. When the time is right. When there are no dreygas around, and we haven't just escaped near-certain death."

I smiled, feeling redness climb to my face despite the tears. "Something to look forward to," I told him. "Unless I kiss you first."

"I dare you," he whispered.

"Accepted."

He smiled and stood, heaving the crystal up again. "Right. Shall we take this to the queen, then?"

"I suppose we should," I sighed, as he hauled me to my

feet with a hand.

Memory served us well, and we retraced our steps back down the hall and through the palace, across the grand foyer with the great wax sculpture, and to the dining room where the queen awaited us. There was someone else there too.

"Oh," Feodor said, looking taken aback. "I wasn't expecting you."

"Yes, well, unexpectedly is always the best time to arrive," Baba Yaga replied. Her black cloak and dress hung down to the floor, long enough to cover her feet and whisper with every movement. I hardly noticed her appearance before, so jarred and frightened after our close call with the dreygas, but in this light, she seemed younger than I remembered. Thick dark waves hung past her shoulders, and her cheekbones were severe enough to make her always seem a little bit angry. There was a beauty to her, the way wild things are beautiful if you let them remain wild.

"Well done to you," Queen Hana said, clasping her hands together. "Well, well done."

I nodded my thanks, too worn out to do much else.

"Let's see it, then," she said, rising from her chair and sweeping around the table.

Feodor heaved the great crystal from the bag and placed it gently on to the tablecloth. A resounding crystalline chime filled the air when it touched the surface.

Baba Yaga ran her hands over it, gently, as if it might

break beneath her touch. "So simple a thing," she said, shaking her head in awe. "Hard to believe it can have such power. Warding off dreygas, holding on to magic…"

"So, it all went to plan," the queen said. "The dreygas arrived, I assume? And Viveka?"

Feodor cleared his throat and began to explain. I shrank away from his words, at the reminder of what was to come, and crossed to a window. The rear gardens were alive with colour, patches of flowers broken by pools of glistening water. A walkway of white stone wound about the vast space, sometimes taking on the form of a small, arched bridge to cross a narrow canal.

There was beauty, so close at hand, and it was worth remembering. As the burden of the past few days – weeks – and the things that had happened today pressed in, filling every inch of space until I could neither see nor breathe, the beauty resting beyond the window offered just enough light and air for me to survive.

"Siya?" Feodor had come to stand behind me. "There's a room ready for you."

I turned to face him, the thought of a bed almost bringing me to my knees. "I'll rest," I told him. "Just for a little while."

I was given the same room as I'd had the first time, the same large bed with the heavy quilts. Feodor left me alone, promising to return later, and in the silence his presence left behind, the screams from the Guild foyer and the shouting of the guards in the Requiem came back. I slipped my face under the blanket, letting the world grow dark, and fought away the memories until sleep grudgingly found me.

I awoke seconds before Feodor tapped on my door. I called for him to enter, and he came in quietly. For the first time since I could remember, he wasn't wearing his coat. Just a dark grey shirt partially tucked into his trousers, his hair more wild than usual.

"You've had a rest," I said, judging by his appearance.

"I did. I thought you might want some company. I thought you might want to … talk about tomorrow." He seated himself at the far end of the bed, twisting to face me with both legs hanging down over the side.

I closed my eyes. "I don't, actually, want to talk about it."

"I know, but… It's best if we do. Without tomorrow, this will be for nothing, Siya."

"You aren't the one who has to do it." I was angry, but tears rose up despite myself. If I had learned anything these past few weeks, it was how closely woven together anger was with sadness.

"I would," he said earnestly, almost pleadingly. "Siya, I would do it for you if I could. I swear to you. But this is one journey which you must take alone. The last one. I promise. I'll be with you for all the others. I won't leave your side again."

"This isn't like any other journey," I told him. Tears ran

252

into the quilts. He reached to wipe one away, but more fell. "I don't want to do it, Feodor, and I – I don't think I can do it. We will have to find another way." There was an edge of begging to my voice. Pleading.

He went quiet for a moment, watching me. "There is no other way, Siya. Our chances for stopping the Guild are slim and small and few. We have to take the chance we have, or it all comes crashing down. Everything we've done. Everything we've worked for. The Guild will never stop coming after us for the pieces of the map, and if they get back to Sarsova, with all of those dreygas… In a matter of weeks – months, years, who knows? – you could be gone. Just, gone." He snapped his fingers. "I don't wish to be in a world without you in it."

A sob rocked my body. Even Feodor's voice was breaking with tears. I could tell he knew how hard it would be, and I believed him when he said he wished he could take my place, but he couldn't. Would I even let him if he could?

"I can't, Feodor. I can't. It's too much. It's too hard. I just need more time."

"There isn't time," he said. "There isn't time, Siya."

His words were a crushing weight, and I sank back beneath the safety of the blankets and cried. There was a shuffling on the bed, and a moment later he was lying beside me, wrapping me in a warm embrace, and though I'd longed for it, I only wished it brought me any comfort.

But the weight of what I had to do hung too heavy, too

oppressive to let any comfort in.

"I can't do it, Feodor," I whispered again. This time, he said nothing.

17

What will they think of me? What will everyone think of me?
And, deep down, how much do I care? Variants of the
same question shadowed me through the dark city. It was
better that I waited until night-time, in case anyone came
looking for me. The cover of darkness offered me some
semblance of safety. Privacy. Let me hide away in the
shadows, so that no one would see what I was about to do.

A phantom embrace from Feodor, the one he had given
me in the bed last night, tickled my arms, and I wrapped
myself in a hug. Things would never be the same after this.
After today. He might never look at me the same way again.
Might never forgive me, really, even if he thought he would.
Even if he thought he wanted this to happen.

Guilt pressed heavily into me, like an ache in every
muscle. Spasms that never let up. With every doorway

I passed, I wanted to slip through it and disappear into darkness. Hide from Feodor. The queen. Baba Yaga. The Guild. Everyone. Write my own map that would take me far away, to a distant and cold island, where I could live alone. Anywhere but here.

I had spent a lot of time wondering what sort of haven I would create for myself if I had magic, and could use it freely. A house by a river, with a chimney and a window and trees. I wanted distant mountains that I could just make out in the distance – just not the Bleaks. I wanted a place where it always snowed, so I could stand outside in the perfect silence it left behind and watch the stars dance. I wanted to never see a city again, right after I saved mine.

Peace, I thought. That was what I really wanted, now that I'd had my adventure. Peace and quiet and endless books, and maybe the occasional adventure that had nothing to do with magic or cities or the Guild.

The dark streets slipped by, one after another, and as I drew closer to my destination, I slowed. I could turn around altogether. Run back to the palace and pretend I had never set out to do this at all. Ease my conscience in any way I could.

Escape.

But in a wandering city, there is nowhere to run.

The shadowed form of the Guild appeared before me when I turned a corner. I stopped.

"You will go through those doors, Siya," I whispered, "and you will see this through to the end. You have come

256

this far." I leaned heavily against the wall of a building, taking in the Guild for as long as I dared. The great doors, the dark, rounded stone walls that rose up, up, up towards the unseeable sky. The few turrets that stood proudly at the very top, flying the flag of magic in the light breeze – white, with the gold map of Shard stitched into the fabric.

Shard, the symbol of magic, of the Guild, the shining diamond of Sarsova.

So fine a thing, a place to learn and honour magic, to understand its strengths and weaknesses, to find new ways to protect the people of Sarsova. So perfect an intention, skewed away into something dark and wicked. Destroyed by a handful of men.

No more time to waste, I told myself, standing up straight again. I stretched my neck. Ready.

I crossed the square and approached the doors with long strides, no longer allowing myself the time to stop and think. No more thinking. No more wondering. I was here now. That was all that mattered.

The Guild doors swept closed behind me, secrets rushing about in their wake.

Only a few souls clung to the Guild at this hour, most returned home for food and rest. But those who had remained were the ones I came to see, the ones whose every waking moment was spent here, spent with magic, spent furthering their plans. A preoccupation that had tipped the scales to delusion. Those were the souls I sought.

The dark foyer was eerily silent, my soft footsteps sounding off the great walls around me. Ahead, the grand staircase beckoned to me, calling me upwards. Up towards where the secrets slept.

I ascended them slowly, deliberately. I would leave here a changed person, if I left here at all. I wanted to savour it, to drink in the good memories I had of this place. The times I had jested with Official Fredek. The stolen moments eavesdropping on conversations not meant for me to hear. The joyous moments that came at the end of the day, when the clock in my dusty study sounded that it was time to return home. That food and company awaited me, and the filing could be put to bed for another day. There were good memories here, hidden amongst the shadows and darker ones, and they were worth holding on to.

I left the staircase on the third floor, knowing the rooms that the Magisters and Officials would haunt. Down the hall, a faint light shone under the doorway of one of their chambers – the same chamber in which Feodor and I had been questioned. It felt so long ago now. And our quest had seemed endless.

But that end was now faintly, barely, in sight.

I clawed my way towards it, pushing all other thoughts aside.

I stopped outside the door, staring at it for a long moment. This was it. This was the moment when I could choose a path. I could still walk away.

My hand drew towards the door, then hung in the air for a moment. My heart thundered, but a sense of purpose had filled my body now, and I was swept along by it. So I tapped three times upon the door, and then pushed it open.

Candlelight met me, along with stunned and silent faces, all seated around a table. Before them were hundreds of parchments, some old and finished, some still being drawn. Large, blank patches of paper still remained. Plans still being made. A globe sat on one end of the table, one of Ermolai's fingers still pointing to something on its surface. But everyone was frozen in place, staring at me.

"Good evening," I greeted them. My voice sounded strong.

"Siya…" my father breathed. He rose, slowly. There were six or seven others in the room – the crux, as Baba Yaga had started to call them. The planners. The ones who knew everything. Had all the plans. Had *made* the plans. There were no secrets between them. Ermolai and my father, and another woman in Magisters' robes. Fredek – though my heart broke to see it – and two other Officials I only knew by name, Henrik and Elitsa.

And Semyon.

My eyes stayed on him for a long while. They must have sensed his malice. His willingness to further himself and magic before ever considering another soul. The arrogance in the room was stifling.

"You are not meant to be here, Siya," my father said, his

259

voice very low. Something in it told me that he would not let me leave this room.

"I know," I replied, and let more silence slip by.

Fredek stepped forward, a hand outstretched to me. His smile was warm and familiar, and I didn't believe it for a second. "I'm glad you've come in of your own accord, Siya," he said. "It was the right thing to do. If you'll just come with me, we'll find you somewhere comfortable to rest while we speak amongst ourselves."

Had this been his way all along? Smiles and friendliness to mask what lay beneath?

"No." The word cut through the room. Fredek withdrew his hand. "I have taken something of yours," I told them, softening. "I think perhaps you have noticed by now. I took something that belonged to you, and I shouldn't have, because it does me no good. I thought it would, but it hasn't. I'm sorry."

I watched them as their eyes darted to each other, hope flickering into life. My father crossed the room to stand before me, leaving very little space between us. His eyes searched mine.

"Siya," he said very slowly. "Do you mean you have…?"

"The crystal," I finished for him. "Yes. The one that protects you all. I have it. I took it from the Requiem. I thought you would have figured that out by now."

My father smiled. He couldn't help himself. Relief flooded his face. "I don't believe her," Semyon said, and the others fell silent, waiting. "She has lied before. Stolen before. She has worked to trip us up at every turn, and now you believe her words yet again? We cannot be fools. We have come too far." He clutched at some of the parchments and held them up as evidence. "Think of what there is to lose."

"You are a Charge, Semyon, and lucky to be privy to these meetings at all. Your silence will do you good here." Ermolai's words were soft, but there was a stern warning behind them.

"Why would she not have brought it with her?" Semyon asked. "Ask her."

"Ask me yourself," I said, through gritted teeth. "Well, for one, I feared thievery. The streets are not what they once were. Fear has begun to run wild. No one knows what to believe. I hid it away from prying eyes, and I dared not carry it around. And secondly, it is remarkably heavy. Hauling it through the city was not possible."

My father and Fredek drew back towards the table, and they all whispered amongst themselves for a moment. My eyes roamed the table, searching for pieces or clues of their work that might jump out, but it was too far away. My palms were damp with sweat, so I rubbed them on my cloak, slowly, waiting.

"What do you want from us?" my father asked suddenly, turning back to face me. "In exchange for the crystal."

I was quiet for a moment. "I want peace when this is all

over," I told him. "When you have your crystal and things are well, I want everything to go back to normal. I want to feel safe. I don't want to work at the Guild any more."

A small, sparkling smile set into my father's face, as though he could so easily agree to what could never be. "Of course, Siya," he said. "Whatever you want."

I nodded. "Then I will take you to it," I said.

"Fredek and Semyon may remain here," Ermolai said, as everyone rose. "Best not to leave the Guild empty."

I stiffened.

"I may not trust her," Semyon said with a touch of offence, "but I'm hardly going to wait behind while you all reach the crystal and get protection first. I think either all of us should go, or none of us."

Fredek sighed and looked at Ermolai. "I do not say this lightly, Ermolai, but I'm inclined to agree with the boy."

I waited without breathing.

After a moment, Ermolai relented. "Very well, then."

My father looked at me. "Is it far?"

"Far enough. I took it somewhere remote. Quiet." I shrugged, a little helplessly. "I didn't know what else to do with it." Playing the fool was easy when they all thought me the fool anyway. The silly, magicless girl who followed them around with a notepad and filed their paperwork.

With soft steps, they all crossed the room to stand before me. And I turned and walked out of the room, the Magisters and Officials following close behind me.

We moved quietly through the Guild, down the stairs, and across the foyer. Whatever chaos had been wrought by the dreygas' visit yesterday had been cleaned up, no trace of it left behind. The screams still echoed about in my mind from time to time, but I had grown better about pushing them away.

"Semyon, the door," my father said, and with a sigh, Semyon heaved open one of the heavy doors and held it open until we had all passed through it. I kept my eyes locked on his as I passed.

"I don't like any of this," he muttered to himself.

You'll like it even less, soon.

Outside, the dark night embraced us. The Guild members cast nervous glances about, clutching their necklaces under their cloaks despite knowing it would do them little good without the crystal they sought. I paused for a moment, remembering the way. Pinpointing the exact street which I needed to take.

There was a narrow street just beyond the bakery in the square. It bore no name, but I knew it was the one. "This way," I told them, and padded across the cobblestones to the small street drenched in shadows.

We walked single-file through the darkness. The occasional whisper of one of the Magisters behind me rose up, but I couldn't make out the words. It didn't matter. They were coming.

The side street ended at a wider road, empty in the late

hour. Behind me, they drew into a cluster, carrying on in their whispering just out of earshot of me. Semyon walked at the back of the group, his arms crossed, distrust rampant on his face whenever I caught a glimpse of him.

A soft sound, like a footstep, echoed nearby. No one seemed to hear it but me, but I paused.

"Siya?" my father said uncertainly.

I hurried forward again. "Yes. Forgive me. I was just remembering the way."

We carried on down the road, until an arched doorway led us into another small street. The buildings towered up on either side, monstrously dark and formidable in the shadow of night. Near the end of the narrow street, an open door led to a staircase going down. I stopped and turned to the others.

"The way is dark from here, but perhaps that is best," I said. "Best not to draw attention to ourselves. We are nearly there."

Far up the way we had just come, behind the group of Guild members, I caught the hint of a shoulder peeking around the corner. It quickly disappeared.

I shivered, and hurried through the door.

The steps were made of uneven stone, so I held on to the walls on both sides as we descended into a long, dark hallway. The air was damp and cold, reaching me despite my cloak. The way seemed carved more than crafted, a tunnel through stone too cold and deep to be anywhere truly in the city. My steps slowed as I realized what that meant. Where we were. I moved to the centre of the hall, turning to walk backwards for a moment to make sure everyone still followed.

"Did you hear something?" Semyon asked, looking over his shoulder. "I think we are being followed. I knew we shouldn't have come."

"Enough, Semyon," Fredek told him, out of breath and holding on to the wall for support. "What would a Clerk be able to do to a group of Magisters and Officials? Use your head, boy. We will be back in the Guild before you know it. Just keep your mouth shut. I beg of you."

Light appeared from a distant opening in the tunnel. Not a golden light, as from a lantern or candles, but the grey-blue light of a night-time lit by stars.

I was doing the right thing, I thought, miserably. It seemed wicked and cruel, but it would save the world. Not every decision is an easy one. I think that was the part that stuck out to me the most. The knowledge that what I was doing, my family might never understand. Never forgive.

I breathed some strength into my being, and I spoke up.

"Wait a moment," I said. I turned to face everyone.

They stopped and looked at me suspiciously. Semyon froze, like a nervous statue.

"What is it?" asked my father.

"I wanted to thank you," I said, my voice bouncing off the stone walls. "I learned more than I thought while I

265

worked at the Guild, even for someone without magic. But incantations and sketches are not the only things to be learned, it turns out. Everything can be useful, if you wait long enough. I learned how to use knowledge I gleaned in just the right way."

My father bowed his head. "I am glad you learned something, at least," he said graciously.

"I did learn," I went on. I turned to walk forward again, my steps slow but long, as though time had slowed down and the seconds were dragging into minutes. "I learned how to twist my knowledge and bend it until I found a way to save the city. Me, a magicless girl who filed papers and citations, finding a way to do something great. Imagine it. I suppose I learned in the end that, *in knowledge lies everything. And in everything, there is magic.*"

As the last words rose up and clung to the cold air, the tunnel ended, and our boots crunched into snow.

The others carried on until everyone had left the tunnel, then stopped moving, silently taking in where we were. Confusion bled into the cold night. Eyes widened. Gasps sounded in the crisp air. A few whispers of *no*. White breaths curled out into the night air from their open mouths. Behind them, the opening of the tunnel disappeared, leaving behind only snow, rocks and stars.

Around us, the Bleaks swept up to the sky, barbed peaks like the teeth of a monster that had swallowed us whole. Dawn was gathering in the east, the burial shroud of night being pulled away by the sun. Nearby, fir trees cloaked in snow clung to the steep slope, the kind of trees that lived only in storybooks since the city had been cursed.

Above, smatterings of stars rested on a blanket of darkness, though some had begun to fade with the growing light. Stars – just like the ones I had dreamed of. Just like the ones that hung above me in the morning hours before I awoke, teasing me, fading further and further from reach as I slowly awoke. But these were real. Real, sparkling stars that would return at night, to smile and keep us company.

The world sat all around me, just like I had dreamed. Snow and trees and rocks and sky and a crisp, cold wind that could only exist in the mountains.

Tears burned my eyes in the cold, and I knelt slowly to brush my fingertips into the snow. Biting cold met me, and I smiled.

"What have you done?" my father breathed.

"I saved Sarsova," I told him, sweeping my arms up to our surroundings. "I saved it from you. From the Guild. From the things you wished to do."

"How do you know about those things?" he snarled. Behind him, Semyon felt frantically around for any hint of the tunnel that might allow him back in. "How would you even be able to understand what we had planned, being what you are? You could never understand it the way we do. Never see the things we see, Siya. What good are you, really? You have no place in the world we want. You would

267

be nothing more than a burden."

Was it anger or sadness that growled to life within me? I supposed it didn't matter.

"You are wrong," I told him. It felt as though I had been waiting years to say those words to him, as all the times that he had brushed me off or muttered that I was useless came thundering back. "You are rotten to your core, Father," I whispered through my teeth. "It is you who have no place in Shard. No place in Sarsova. Not me. Not others like me."

He scoffed.

I remembered the words of the librarian. About how books were his magic. "This is my magic," I told him. "Knowledge. Resourcefulness. Immunity to dreygas."

"You are a fool, Anastasiya," he breathed, shaking his head.

"And anyway," I went on, "you don't need magic to see the wickedness in murder." I stepped closer, so I could see his face clearly. "You don't need magic to understand what is good and what is evil. And you, Father, you are evil. Evil with flesh and bone, and the only way to stop you, is to end you. All of you."

"It wouldn't have been murder!" my father cried, throwing his hands into the air furiously. "You wouldn't even have known what happened. None of you would have. Simply a new map, and a new world, created with all the magic stored up in the crystal. Painstakingly gathered, through great sacrifice. The old world washed away, as though it had never been there at all." He snapped his fingers. "No pain at all. A world designed the way the First Enchanters intended it, built for magic, by magic, where magic can run free. Where the Guild is in charge of everything, as it should be. Not just Shard. Because without magic, Anastasiya, what purpose do you serve in this world? What greater existence do you aspire to? There is *nothing* for you. A meaningless life, and then death. We can change all of that. Build a world where magic is *everything*. *Everywhere*. Without the king of Sarsova, without the church, without—"

"Baba Yaga," I finished for him. "Yes. You have her to thank for this." I turned to take in the sweeping dawn views. "She worked the map to lead us here. She permitted the city to go back to Sarsova. Back to the Bleaks. Just long enough to send you all out into the wilderness, running wild with the dreygas. There are many of them here, I'm told. Hundreds. Thousands. And they cannot leave the mountains because of map magic, so they are trapped here with you." I laughed a little. "I had always wanted to see mountains too. I suppose some dreams do come true." I turned back to him. "Just not yours."

Ermolai started forward, as if to strangle me, but stopped suddenly, his eyes shifting to something behind me. Silence swept over the group like a wave, leaving horror behind. I turned slowly, knowing what I would find when I did.

Tall, graceful forms melted from the snow and shadows

269

around us. Golden-orange eyes pierced the darkness, eyeing their prey hungrily, curiously. The prey I had so carefully delivered to them. Ragged grey clothing clung to their frames, waving in the mountain breeze. They stared as if they couldn't trust their eyes, more magical bodies lingering before them than they had ever seen in one place.

I turned back to my father. "You have your dreygas," I told him, sweeping an arm to them. "As many as you want." One of the dreygas brushed past my shoulder, uninterested in me and my lack of magic. It drew close to my father's face, hissing softly. Something in me started to break.

"Siya," my father said, his eyes glassy with fear.

"Father," I whispered back, tears burning my eyes in the cold. "I'm sorry." I turned away, unable to watch what would happen next, and started my long walk down the mountains. "I'm sorry you couldn't have been better."

The snow crunching beneath my boots and the wind that rushed past my ears drowned out just enough of the screams as I descended away, away, away.

The sun had long ago risen, sending diamonds along the snow. My journey was slow, due mostly to my frequent stops to stare at the sky, to turn and admire the mountains, to run my hands along the bark of the trees and drink in the way it felt beneath my fingers. There was a war within me, half recoiling at the knowledge of what I had just done, the deaths I had just brought about, and the other half alive in a way it had never been before, drinking in every beautiful sight, every new rock, every cloud that hung lazily in the morning sky.

This was the world, bright and alive and beautiful. Broken and rare and dazzling. There was a sadness in knowing that years of our lives had been stripped away while we were bound to a cursed city, captives to an evil that we didn't fully understand. To a darkness that had festered beneath the surface of the city we loved, like the spark of a fire we couldn't see until it had set the world on fire.

But all that was gone now. Evil would linger in the world, as it always would, but the dark designs of the Guild, of my father and Feodor's father and the others, those were gone. Burned away. Evil fed to evil that would stay locked away in the mountains.

And soon enough, Farod and the other dreyga would join their companions, sent to the Bleaks by Baba Yaga, to live out the rest of their innumerable days.

The craggy peaks of the Bleaks soon fell away as I carried on my descent, a curtain drawn to reveal a sparkling valley below. The snow vanished ahead, melting into green and blue where rivers ran down to meet a distant lake. Far away, miniature curls of smoke rose into the sky from a far-off town – a town I'd never been to, filled with people I had never met. Brimming with newness, a hundred possibilities contained within.

I stopped to soak it in, the mountains surrounding me,

the trees that stood as towers clustered about the land, the valley of ice-bound dreams before me, holding things I had only touched in the pages of a book. Places I had built in my mind. Never real. I rubbed tears from my eyes with my palms and dropped to sit on a rock, the wind and the sun and the view all too much. I wished never to move from this spot, dreygas or no dreygas. I wished to sit here for ever and let the sweeping view of my beloved Sarsova consume me for all of my days.

But as a shimmer took form in the valley below, I was reminded of those who waited for me.

My own true family waited too, and I would have to tell them of the things that had happened. The things I had done. And most importantly, why. Unravel for them the tangled mess that had become the Guild over the years, and hope that with time, they would see that I had done the right thing.

If I could first convince myself.

The shimmer soon gave way to walls and towers and gates, and in a vast expanse of emptiness below, the City of Shard eased into being. It settled into the world around it as though it had never left, a dragon easing down for a nap in its mountain after a long and winding journey. A homecoming, at last.

After the Guild had been emptied of those I had brought to the mountains, Baba Yaga had gathered up the last piece of the map they had kept framed, and matched it with the one Feodor and I had stolen and the one that the queen kept, breaking our curse and bringing us home.

So I rose and wiped the tears away. With a certainty that slipped on like a glove, I let my feet take me down the mountain and into the valley, where cracks of daylight could at last shine through all of the dark places that evil had left behind.

The gates had been raised as I had approached – Baba Yaga likely watching from a tower to ensure that everything had gone according to plan. That the crux of the Guild was gone. That I was alone.

I stopped a short walk from the gates to watch as people filtered out, slowly, staring mostly up at the sky. A few bore the expression of someone sceptical, wondering if they were perhaps trapped in a dream. If they would awaken to find the city still cursed. Some dropped to their hands and knees and clutched at the remnants of snow left in the shadows, the snow a cold and distant dawn had not melted away. There were cries ringing all through the crisp morning air, and I felt certain that if I heard enough of it, it would eventually fix the parts of me that had broken in the mountains.

Then, from the gates, a familiar face emerged. A long red coat and a mess of hair and the kind of smile that could melt snow. I started to move, then stopped as his feet quickened, letting him cross the distance to me. He took a full turn as he walked, taking in the land and the air and the sky with his arms stretched up, as though it had been everything he had dreamed of and refused to let himself hope for.

"Siya!" he cried, sweeping towards me and slipping on hidden ice. I tried to keep him from falling, but we ended up tumbling to the ground together, laughing. "We're here," he whispered as I rested my head on his shoulder. "We're back."

"We're back," I told him. "It's done."

He drew back and looked into my eyes, searching for the pain that I struggled to keep buried. "Are you all right?" he asked, taking my face in both hands. He knew what I'd had to do. Knew how hard it would be to face, and to face alone. He hadn't wished for this end any more than I had, but we both knew it was the only way. To keep their evil from springing up, again and again.

"Yes," I told him, watching two children run through the gates, shrieking with joy as their mother tried to chase them. "And no." My eyes burned with tears again, but everything I felt was too tangled and messy to understand, joy mingling with fear and hurt until all I felt was one great, overwhelming emotion that was too heavy to bear. I shook my head, over and over again, as Feodor pulled me back in for an embrace.

"Shh," he said softly, as we stared off towards the smoke of distant chimneys and clusters of trees dressed in snow that was slowly melting away in the sunlight. "Don't think on it now. Just sit, and rest, and remember all the good things you have brought to your people. Listen to them laugh, and talk, and play, and save everything else for another time."

Feodor was right. There was so much joy around us as faces continued to emerge from the city, tears shed, laughter ringing out through the valley. This was joy, and this was beauty, and this was goodness. It had been worth fighting for. Shard belonged here, in its valley below the mountains where it had sat for centuries.

Shard was home.

And the sunlight burned away all of the shadows that the Guild had left behind, filling every crack and broken place with the warm and golden glow of hope. So we sat for a while, letting the light of this new crystalline world soak into our hearts. My father was gone. Feodor's father was gone. But a goodness had been born in their place that would echo through generations to come, and that, I told myself, mattered more than anything.

I turned to Feodor, squinting against the harsh light, and took his face in my hands. "I'll take that kiss now," I told him.

ACKNOWLEDGEMENTS

Thank you to:

My agent, Silvia Molteni, my editor, Sophie Cashell, and to everyone at Scholastic who has made this book possible.

My husband, Thomas, and my son, Atlas, for being there for me every single day.

Thank you to the greatest family that anyone could ask for.

Thank you to everyone who has read my books. I'm so thankful for you.

And thank you to coffee, because without coffee, I'm fairly certain that there would be no book.

LISA LUEDDECKE

the
FOREST
of
GHOSTS
and
BONES

Enter a world with a haunted castle, a dark and
dangerous forest and poisoned rain…